# MYTH-ING PERSONS

# MYTH-ING PERSONS

# ROBERT ASPRIN

## Illustrated by Phil Foglio

**The Donning Company/Publishers**
Norfolk/Virginia Beach

Starblaze Editions

Edited by Kay Reynolds

*Other titles in this series:*
**Another Fine Myth**
**Myth Conceptions**
**Myth Directions**
**Hit or Myth**
**Myth-ing Persons** is one of the many fantasy and
science fiction titles published by The Donning
Company/Publishers. For a complete listing of our titles,
please write to the address below.

**The Donning Company/Publishers**
**5659 Virginia Beach Boulevard**
**Norfolk, Virginia 23502**

10 9 8 7 6 5 4 3 2 1

**Library of Congress Cataloging in Publication Data:**

Asprin, Robert.
    Myth-ing Persons.

    I. Title.
PS3551.S6M94    1984        813'.54        84-13824
ISBN 0-89865-380-0 (hard)
ISBN 0-89865-379-7 (trade)
ISBN 0-89865-381-9 (lim.ed.)

Cover and illustrations copyright © 1984 Phil Foglio

**Printed in the United States of America**

# Chapter I

*"Reputations are fine up to a point.*
*After that they become a pain!"*
**D. Juan**

THERE is something sinfully satisfying about doing something you know you aren't supposed to. This was roughly my frame of mind as I approached a specific nondescript tent at the Bazaar at Deva with my breakfast under my arm...guilty, but smug.

"Excuse me, young sahr!"

I turned to find an elderly Deveel waving desperately at me as he hurried forward. Normally I would have avoided the encounter, as Deveels are always selling something and at the moment I wasn't buying, but since I wasn't in a hurry I decided to hear what he had to say.

"I'm glad I caught you in time," he said, struggling to catch his breath. "While I don't usually meddle, you really don't want to go in there!"

"Why not? I was just...."

"Do you know who lives there?"

"Well, actually I thought...."

"That is the dwelling of the Great Skeeve!"

1

Something about this busybody irritated me. Maybe it was the way he never let me finish a sentence. Anyway, I decided to string him along for a while."

"The Great Skeeve?"

"You never heard of him?" The Deveel seemed genuinely shocked. "He's probably the most powerful magician at the Bazaar."

My opinion of the busybody soared to new heights, but the game was too much fun to abandon.

"I've never had too much faith in magicians," I said with studied casualness. "I've found for the most part their powers are overrated."

The oldster rolled his eyes in exasperation.

"That may be true in most cases, but not when it comes to the Great Skeeve! Did you know he consorts with Demons and has a dragon for a familiar?"

I favored him with a worldly smile.

"So what? Deva is a crossroads of the dimensions. Dimension travelers, or Demons as you call them, are the norm around here. As a Deveel, your main livelihood comes from dealing with Demons. As for the dragon, there's a booth not eight rows from here that sells dragons to anyone with the price."

"No, no! You don't understand! Of course we all deal with Demons when it comes to business. The difference is that this Skeeve is actually *friends* with them...invites them into his home and lives with them. One of his permanent house guests is a Pervert, and I don't know of a single Deveel who would stoop that low. What's more, I've heard it said that he has underworld connections."

The game was growing tiresome. Any points the Deveel had made with his tribute to the Great Skeeve had been lost with interest when he started commenting on Demons.

"Well, thank you for your concern," I said, holding out my hand for a handshake. "I promise you I'll remember everything you've said. What was your name again?"

2

The Deveel grabbed my hand and began pumping it vigorously.

"I am Aliman, and glad to be of assistance," he said with an ingratiating smile. "If you really want to show your gratitude, remember my name. Should you ever be in need of a *reputable* magician, I have a nephew who's just getting started in the business. I'm sure we could arrange some discount prices for you. Tell me, what is *your* name so I can tell him who to watch for?"

I tightened my grip slightly and gave him my widest smile. "Well, my friends call me Skeeve."

"I'll be sure to tell...SKEEVE?"

The Deveel's eyes widened, and his complexion faded from red to a delicate pink.

"That's right," I said, retaining my grip on his hand. "Oh, and for your information Demons from Perv are called Pervects, not Perverts...and he's not my house guest, he's my partner."

The Deveel was struggling desperately now, trying to free his hand.

"Now then, how many customers have you scared away from my business with your tales about what a fearsome person I am?"

The Deveel tore loose from my grip and vanished into the crowds, sounding an incoherent scream of terror as he went. In short, Aliman left. Right?

I watched him go with a certain amount of mischievous satisfaction. I wasn't really angry, mind you. We literally had more money than we could use right now, so I didn't begrudge him the customers. Still, I had never really paused to consider how formidable our operation must look from the outside. Viewing it now through a stranger's eyes, I found myself more than a little pleased. Considering the dubious nature of my beginning, we had built ourselves quite a reputation over the last few years.

I had been serious when I told Aliman that I didn't have much faith in magicians. My own reputation was overrated to say the least, and if I was being billed as a powerful magician, it made the others of my profession more than a little suspect in my eyes. After several years of seeing the inside of the magic business, I was starting to wonder if *any* magician was really as good as people thought.

I was so wrapped up in these thoughts as I entered our humble tent that I had completely forgotten that I was supposed to be sneaking in. I was reminded almost immediately.

The reminder came in the form of a huge man who loomed up to block my path. "Boss," he said in a squeaky little voice that was always surprising coming from such a huge body, "you shouldn't ought to go out alone like that. How many times we got to tell you...."

"It's all right, Nunzio," I said, trying to edge around him. "I just ducked out to get some breakfast. Want a bagel?"

Nunzio was both unconvinced and undaunted in his scolding.

"How are we supposed to be your bodyguards if you keep sneaking off alone every chance you get? Do you know what Don Bruce would do to us if anything happened to you?"

"C'mon, Nunzio. You know how things are here at the Bazaar. If the Deveels see me with a bodyguard, the price of everything goes through the ceiling. Besides, I like being able to wander around on my own once in a while."

"You can afford the higher prices. What you can't afford is to set yourself up as a target for every bozo who wants the rep of bagging the Great Skeeve."

I started to argue, but my conversation with Aliman flashed across my mind. Nunzio was right. There were two sides to having a reputation. If anyone believed the rumors at the Bazaar and still meant me harm, they would muster such firepower for the attempt that my odds for survival would be nonexistent.

"Nunzio," I said slowly, "you may be right, but in all honesty what could you and Guido do to stop a magical attack on me?"

"Not a thing," he said calmly. "But they'd probably try to knock off your bodyguards first, and that might give you time to get away or hit them yourself before they could muster a second attack."

He said it easily, like you or I might say "The sun rises in the east," but it shook me. It had never really occurred to me how expendable bodyguards are, or how readily they accept the dangers of their profession.

"I'll try to remember that in the future," I said with a certain degree of grave humility. "What's more, I think I owe you and Guido an apology. Where is Guido, anyway?"

"Upstairs arguing with His Nibbs," Nunzio grinned. "As a matter of fact, I was looking for you to break it up when I found you had snuck out again."

"Why didn't you say so in the first place?"

"What for? There's no rush. They'll be arguing until you get there. I figured it was more important to convince you to quit going out alone."

I groaned a little inside, but I had learned long ago the futility of arguing priorities with Nunzio.

"Well, thanks again for the advice, but I'd better get upstairs before those two kill each other."

With that I headed across the courtyard for the fountain stairs to our offices....

Courtyard? Fountain stairs?

What happened to the humble tent I was walking into a minute ago?

*Weelll*...I said I was a magician, didn't I? Our little stall at the Bazaar is bigger on the inside than it is on the outside. Lots bigger. I've lived in royal palaces that weren't as big as our "humble tent." I can't take any credit for this particular miracle, though, other than the fact that it was my work that helped earn us our current residence. We live here rent-free courtesy of the Devan

5

Merchants Association as partial payment for a little job we did for them a while back. That's also how I got my bodyguards...but that's another story.

Devan Merchants Association, you ask? Okay. For the uninitiated, I'll go over this just once. The dimension I'm currently residing in is Deva, home of the shrewdest deal-drivers in all the known dimensions. You may have heard of them. In my own home dimension they were called devils, but I have since learned the proper pronunciation is Deveels. Anyway, my gracious living quarters are the result of my partner and I beating the Deveels at their own game...which is to say we got the better of them in a deal. Don't tell anyone, though. It would ruin their reputation and maybe even cost me a cushy spot. You see, they still don't know they've been had.

Anyway, where was I? Oh, yes. Heading for the offices. Normally after sneaking out I would stop by the stables to share breakfast with Gleep, but with a crisis on my hands I decided to forgo the pleasure of my pet's company and get to work. Gleep. He's the dragon Aliman was talking about...and I'm *not* going to try to condense *that* story. It's just too complicated.

Long before I reached the offices I could hear their voices raised in their favorite "song." The lyrics changed from time to time, but I knew the melody by heart.

"Incompetent bungler!"

"Who are you calling an incomplete bungler?"

"I stand corrected. You are a *complete* bungler!"

You better watch your mouth! Even if you are the boss's partner, one more word and I'll...."

"You'll what? If you threw a punch the safest place to be would be where you're aiming."

"Izzat so?"

It sounded like I had arrived in the nick of time. Taking a deep breath, I casually strolled into the teeth of the fracas.

"Hi, guys." I pretended to be totally unaware of what

6

was going on. "Anyone want a bagel?"

"No, I don't want a bagel!" came the sneering response from one combatant. "What I want is some decent help."

"...and while you're at it see what you can do about getting me a little respect!" the other countered.

The latter comment came from Guido, senior of my two bodyguards. If anything, he's bigger and nastier than his cousin Nunzio.

The former contribution came from Aahz. Aahz is my partner. He's also a demon, a Pervect to be exact, and even though he's slightly shorter than I am, he's easily twice as nasty as my two bodyguards put together.

My strategy had worked in that I now had their annoyance focused on me instead of each other. Now, realizing the potential devastation of their respective temperaments individually, much less collectively, I had cause to doubt the wisdom of my strategy.

"What seems to be the trouble?"

"The trouble," Aahz snarled, "is that your ace body-guard here just lost us a couple of clients."

My heart sank. I mentioned earlier that Aahz and I have more money than we know what to do with, but old habits die hard. Aahz is the tightest being I've ever met when it comes to money, and, living at the Bazaar at Deva, that's saying something! If Guido had really lost a potential customer, we'd be hearing about it for a long time.

"Ease up a minute, partner," I said more to stall for time than anything else. "I just got here, remember? Could you fill me in on a few of the details?"

Aahz favored Guido with one more dark stare.

"There's not all that much to tell," he said. "I was in the middle of breakfast..."

"He was drinking another meal," Guido translated scornfully.

"...when mush-for-brains here bellows up that there are some customers waiting downstairs in reception. I called back that I'd be down in a few, then finished my meal."

"He kept them waiting at least half an hour. You can't expect customers to. . . ."

"Guido, could you hold the editorial asides for one round? Please?" I interceded before Aahz could go for him. "I'm still trying to get a rough idea of what happened, remember? Okay, Aahz. You were saying?"

Aahz took a deep breath, then resumed his account.

"Anyway, when I got downstairs, the customers were nowhere to be seen. You'd think your man here would be able to stall them or at least have the sense to call for reinforcements if they started getting twitchy."

"C'mon, Aahz. Guido is supposed to be a bodyguard, not a receptionist. If some customers got tired of waiting for you to show up and left, I don't see where you can dodge the blame by shifting it to. . . ."

"Wait a minute, Boss. You're missing the point. They didn't leave!"

"Come again?"

"I left 'em there in the reception room, and the next thing I know Mr. Mouth here is hollerin' at me for losing customers. They never came out! Now, like you say, I'm supposed to be a bodyguard. By my figuring we've got some extra people wandering the premises, and all this slob wants to do is yell about whose fault it is."

"I know whose fault it is," Aahz said with a glare. "There are only two ways out of that reception room, and they didn't come past me!"

"Well they didn't come past *me*!" Guido countered.

I started to get a very cold feeling in my stomach.

"Aahz," I said softly.

"If you think I don't know when. . . ."

"AAHZ!"

That brought him up short. He turned to me with an angry retort on his lips, then he saw my expression.

"What is it, Skeeve? You look as if. . . ."

"There are more than two ways out of that room."

We stared at each other in stunned silence for a few moments, then we both sprinted for the reception room, leaving Guido to trail along behind.

The room we had selected for our reception area was one of the largest in the place, and the only large room with easy access from the front door. It was furnished in a style lavish enough to impress even those customers spoiled by the wonders of the Bazaar who were expecting to see the home office of a successful magician. There was only one problem with it, and that was the focus of our attention as we dashed in.

The only decoration that we had kept from the previous owners was an ornate tapestry hanging on the north wall. Usually I'm faster than Aahz, but this time he beat me to the hanging, sweeping it aside with his arm to reveal a heavy door behind it.

Our worst fears were realized.

The door was unlocked and standing ajar.

# Chapter II

*"Success often hinges on
choosing a reliable partner."*
**Remus**

WHAT'S THAT?" Guido demanded, taking advantage of our stunned silence.

"It's a door," I said.

"An open door, to be specific," Aahz supplied.

" I can see that for myself!" the bodyguard roared. "I meant what is it doing here?"

"It would look pretty silly standing alone in the middle of the street now, wouldn't it?" Aahz shot back.

Guido purpled. As I've said, these two have a positive talent for getting under each other's skins.

"Now look, all I'm askin'. . . . "

"Guido, could you just hang on for a few minutes until we decide what to do next? Then we'll explain, I promise."

My mind was racing over the problem, and having Aahz and Guido going at each other did nothing for my concentration.

"I think the first thing we should do, partner," Aahz said thoughtfully, "is to get the door closed so that we won't be. . .interrupted while we work this out."

10

Rather than answer, I reached out a cautious toe and pushed the door shut. Aahz quickly slipped two of the bolts in place to secure it.

That done, we leaned against the door and looked at each other in silence.

"Well? What do you think?" I asked at last.

"I'm in favor of sealing it up again and forgetting the whole thing."

"Think it's safe to do that?"

"Don't know, really. Not enough information."

We both turned slowly to level thoughtful stares at Guido.

"Say, uh, Guido, could you tell us a little more about those customers who came in this morning?"

"Nothing doin'." Guido crossed his arms. "You're the guys who insist on 'information for information.' Right? Well, I'm not telling you anything more until somebody tells me about that door. I mean, I'm supposed to be your bodyguard and nobody bothers to tell me there's another way into this place?"

Aahz bared his teeth and started forward, but I caught him by the shoulder.

"He's right, partner. If we want his help, we owe him an explanation."

We locked eyes again for a moment, then he shrugged and retreated.

"Actually, Guido, the explanation is very simple...."

"That'll be a first," the bodyguard grumbled.

In a bound, Aahz was across the room and had Guido by the shirt front.

"You wanted an explanation? Then SHUT UP AND LET HIM EXPLAIN!"

Now Guido is no lightweight, and he's never been short in the courage department. Still, there's nothing quite like Aahz when he's really mad.

"O—Okay! Sorry! Go ahead, Boss. I'm listening."

Aahz released his grip and returned to his place by

11

the door, winking at me covertly as he went.

"What happened is this," I said, hiding a smile. "Aahz and I found that door when we first moved in here. We didn't like the looks of it, so we decided to leave it alone. That's all."

"That's all!? A back door that even you admit looks dangerous and all you do is ignore it? And if that wasn't bad enough, you don't even bother to tell your bodyguards about it? Of all the lamebrained, half...."

Aahz cleared his throat noisily, and Guido regained control of himself...rapidly.

"Aahh...what I mean to say is...oh well. That's all behind us now. Could you give *me* a little more information now that the subject's out in the open? What's on the other side of that door, anyway?"

"We don't know," I admitted.

"YOU DON'T KNOW?" Guido shrieked.

"What we *do* know," Aahz interrupted hastily, "is what *isn't* on the other side. What isn't there is any dimension we know about."

Guido blinked, then shook his head. "I don't get it. Could you run that past me again...real slow?"

"Let me try," I said. "Look, Guido, you already know about dimensions, right? How we're living in the dimension Deva, which is an entirely different world than our own home dimension of Klah? Well, the people here, the Deveels, are masters of dimension travel to a point where they build their houses across the dimension barriers. That's how come this place is bigger on the inside than it is on the outside. The door is in Deva, but the rest of the house is in another dimension. That means if we go through that door, the back door that we've just shown you, we'd be in another world...one we know nothing about. That's why we were willing to leave it sealed up rather than stick our noses out into a completely un-known situation."

"I still think you should have checked it out," the

bodyguard insisted stubbornly.

"Think again," Aahz supplied. "You've only seen two dimensions. Skeeve here has visited a dozen. I've been to over a hundred myself. The Deveels you see here at the Bazaar, on the other hand, know over a thousand different dimensions."

"So?"

"So we think they gave us this place because it opens into a dimension that *they* don't want... 'don't want' as in 'scared to death of'. Now, you've seen what a Deveel will brave to turn a profit. Do *you* want to go exploring in a world that's too mean for *them* to face?"

"I see what you mean."

"Besides," Aahz finished triumphantly, "take another look at that door. It's got more locks and bolts than three ordinary bank vaults."

"*Somebody* opened it," Guido said pointedly.

That took some of the wind out of Aahz's sails. Despite himself, he shot a nervous glance at the door.

"Well... a good thief with a lockpick working from this side...."

"Some of these locks weren't picked, Aahz."

I had been taking advantage of their discussion to do a little snooping, and now held up one of my discoveries for their inspection. It was a padlock with the metal shackle snapped off. There were several of them scattered about, as if someone had gotten impatient with the lockpick and simply torn the rest of them apart with his hands.

Guido pursed his lips in a silent whistle. "Man, that's strong. What kind of person could to that?"

"That's what we've been trying to get you to tell us," Aahz said nastily. "Now, if you don't mind, what were those customers like?"

"Three of them... two men and a woman... fairly young-looking, but nothing special. Klahds by the look of 'em. Come to think of it, they did seem a bit nervous, but I thought it was just because they were coming to see a magician."

"Well, now they're on the other side of the door." Aahz scooped up one of the undamaged locks and snapped it into place. "I don't think they can pick locks, or break them if they can't reach 'em. They're there, which is their problem, self-inflicted I might add, and we're here. End of puzzle. End of problem."

"Do you really think so, Aahz?"

"Trust me."

Somehow that phrase struck a familiar chord in my memory, and the echoes weren't pleasant. I was about to raise this point with Aahz when Nunzio poked his head in the door.

"Hey, Boss. You got visitors."

"See?" my partner exclaimed, beaming. "I told you things could only get better! It's not even noon and we've got more customers."

"Actually," Nunzio clarified, "it's a delegation of Deveels. I think it's the landlord."

"The landlord?" Aahz echoed hollowly.

"See how much better things have gotten?" I said with a disgusted smirk. "And it's not even noon."

"Shall I run 'em off, Boss?" Guido suggested.

"I think you'd better see 'em," Nunzio advised. "They seem kind'a upset. Something about us harboring fugitives."

Aahz and I locked gazes in silence, which was only natural as there was nothing more to be said. With a vague wave that bordered on a nervous tick, I motioned for Nunzio to show the visitors in.

As expected, it was the same delegation of four from the Devan Chamber of Commerce who had originally hired us to work for the Bazaar, headed by our old adversary, Hay-ner. Last time we dealt with him, we had him over a barrel and used the advantage mercilessly. While he had agreed to our terms, I always suspected it had hurt his Devan pride to cut such a generous deal and that he

14

had been waiting ever since to pay us back. From the smile on his face as he entered our reception room, it appeared he felt his chance had finally come.

"Aahh, Master Skeeve," he said. "How good of you to see us so promptly without an appointment. I know how busy you are, so I'll come right to the point. I believe there are certain individuals in residence here that our organization is *most* anxious to speak with. If you would be so kind as to summon them, we won't trouble you further."

"Wait a minute, Hay-ner," Aahz put in before I could respond. "What makes you think the people you're looking for are here?"

"Because they were seen entering your tent less than an hour ago and haven't come out yet," said the largest of Hay-ner's back-up team.

I noticed that unlike Hay-ner, he wasn't smiling. In fact, he looked down-right angry.

"He must mean the ones who came in earlier," Nunzio suggested helpfully. "You know, Boss, the two guys with the broad."

Aahz rolled his eyes in helpless frustration, and for once I was inclined to agree with him.

"Umm, Nunzio," I said, staring at the ceiling. "why don't you and Guido wait outside while we take care of this?"

The two bodyguards trooped outside in silence, though I noticed that Guido glared at his cousin with such disdain that I suspected a stern dressing-down would take place even before I could get to him myself. The Mob is no more tolerant than magicians of staff members who say more than they should in front of the opposition.

"Now that we've established that we all know who we're talking about and that they're here," Hay-ner said, rubbing his hands together, "call them out and we'll finish this once and for all."

"Not so fast," I interrupted. "First of all, neither of us have laid eyes on those folks you're looking for, because, second of all, they aren't here. They took it on the lam out the back door before we could meet them."

"Somehow, I don't expect you to take our word for it," Aahz added. "So feel free to search the place."

The Deveel's smile broadened, and I was conscious of cold sweat breaking out on my brow.

"That won't be necessary. You see, whether I believe you or not is of little consequence. Even if we searched, I'm sure you would be better at hiding things than we would be at finding them. All that really matters is that we've established that they did come in here, and that makes them *your* responsibility."

I wasn't sure exactly what was going on here, but I *was* sure that I was liking it less and less with each passing moment.

"Wait a minute, Hay-ner," I began. "What do you mean 'We're responsible'? Responsible for what?"

"Why, for the fugitives, of course. Don't you remember? When we agreed to let you use this place rent-free, part of the deal was that if anyone of this household broke any of the Bazaar rules, and either disappeared off to another dimension or otherwise refused to face the charges, that you would personally take responsibility for their actions. It's a standard clause in any Bazaar lease."

"Aahz," I said testily, "you cut the deal. Was there a clause like that in it?"

"There was," he admitted. "But I was thinking of Tananda and Chumley at the time...and we'll stand behind them anytime. Massha, too. It never occurred to me that they'd try to claim that anyone who walked through our door was a member of our household. I don't see how they can hope to prove...."

"We don't have to prove that they're in your household," Hay-ner smiled. "You have to prove they aren't."

"That's crazy," Aahz exploded. "How can we prove...."

"Can it, Aahz. We can't prove it. That's the point. All

16

right, Hay-ner. You've got us. Now what exactly have these characters done that we're responsible for and what are our options? I thought one of the big sales points of the Bazaar was that there weren't any rules here."

"There aren't many," the Deveel said, "but the few that do exist are strictly enforced. The specific rule your friends broke involves fraud."

He quickly held up a hand to suppress my retort.

"I know what you're going to say. Fraud sounds like a silly charge with all the hard bargaining that goes on here at the Bazaar, but to us it's a serious matter. While we pride ourselves in driving a hard bargain, once the deal is made you get the goods you were promised. Sometimes there are specific details omitted in describing the goods, but anything actually *said* is true. That is our reputation and the continued success of the Bazaar depends on that reputation being scrupulously maintained. If a trader or merchant sells something claiming it to be magical and it turns out to have no powers at all, that's fraud...and if the perpetrators are allowed to go unpunished, it could mean the end of the Bazaar as we know it."

"Actually," I said drily, "all I was going to do was protest you billing them as our friends, but I'll let it go. What you haven't mentioned is our options."

Hay-ner shrugged. "There are only three, really. You can pay back the money they took falsely plus a twenty-five percent fine, accept permanent banishment from the Bazaar, or you can try to convince your fr—aahh, I mean the fugitives to return to the Bazaar to settle matters themselves."

"I see.... Very well. You've had your say. Now please leave so my partner and I can discuss our position on the matter."

Aahz took care of seeing them out while I plunged into thought as to what we should do. When he returned, we both sat in silence for the better part of an hour before either of us spoke.

"Well," I said at last, "what do you think?"

"Banishment from the Bazaar is out!" Aahz snarled. "Not only would it destroy our reputations, I'm not about to get run out of the Bazaar *and* our home over something as idiotic as this!"

"Agreed," I said grimly. "Even though it occurs to me that Hay-ner is bluffing on that option. He wants us to stick around the Bazaar as much as we want to stay. He was the one who hired us in the first place, remember? I think he's expecting us to ante up and pay the money. That way he gets back some of the squeeze he so grudgingly parted with. Somehow the idea of giving in to that kind of pressure really galls me."

Aahz nodded. "Me too."

There followed several more minutes of silence.

"Okay," Aahz said finally, "who's going to say it?"

"We're going to have to go after them." I sighed.

"Half right," Aahz corrected. "*I'm* going to have to go after them. Partner or not, we're talking about hitting a totally new dimension here, and it's too dangerous for someone at your level of magical skill."

"*My* level? How about you? You don't have any powers at all. If it's too dangerous for me, what's supposed to keep you safe?"

"Experience," he said loftily. "I'm used to doing this, and you aren't. End of argument."

"'End of argument' nothing! Just how to you propose to leave me behind if I don't agree?"

"That's easy," Aahz grinned. "See who's standing in the corner?"

I turned to look where he was pointing, and that's the last thing I remembered for a long time.

# Chapter III

*"Reliable information is a must
for successful planning."*
C. Columbus

HEY! Hot stuff! Wake up!! You okay?"

If I led a different kind of life, those words would have been uttered by a voluptuous vision of female loveliness. As it was, they were exclaimed by Massha.

This was one of the first things that penetrated the fogginess of my mind as I struggled to regain consciousness. I'm never at my best first thing in the morning, even when I wake up leisurely of my own accord. Having wakefulness forced upon me by someone else only *guarantees* that my mood will be less than pleasant.

However groggy I might be feeling, though, there was no mistaking the fact that it was Massha shaking me awake. Even through unfocused eyes, her form was unmistakable. Imagine, if you will, the largest, fattest woman you've ever met. Now expand that image by fifty percent in all directions, top it off with garish orange hair, and false eyelashes and purple lipstick, and adorn it with a wheelbarrow load of gaudy jewelry. See what I mean? I could recognize Massha a mile away on a dark night . . . blindfolded.

"Of course I'm okay, *apprentice*!" I snarled. "Don't you have any lessons you're supposed to be practicing or something?"

"Are you *sure*?" she pressed mercilessly.

"Yes, I'm sure. Why do you ask? Can't a fellow take a little nap without being badgered about it?"

"It's just that you don't usually take naps in the middle of the reception room floor."

That got my attention, and I forced my eyes into focus. She was right! For some reason I was sprawled out on the floor. Now what could have possessed me to. . . .

Then it all came back! Aahz! The expedition into the new dimension!

I sat bolt upright. . .and regretted it immediately. A blinding headache assaulted me with icepick intensity, and my stomach flipped over and landed on its back with all the grace of a lump of overcooked oatmeal.

Massha caught me by the shoulder as I started to list.

"Steady there, High Roller. Looks like your idea of 'okay' and mine are a little out of synch."

Ignoring her, I felt the back of my head cautiously and discovered a large, tender lump behind my ear. If I had had any doubts as to what had happened, they were gone now.

"That bloody Pervert!" I said, flinching at the new wave of pain brought on by the sound of my own voice. "He must have knocked me out and gone in alone!"

"You mean Aahz? Dark, green, and scaly himself? I don't get it. Why would your own partner sucker-punch you?"

"So he could go through the door without me. I made it very clear that I didn't want to be left behind on this caper."

"Door? What door?" Massha said with a frown. "I know you two have your secrets, Boss, but I think you'd better fill me in on a few more details as to exactly what's going on around here."

As briefly as I could, I brought her up to date on the

day's events, including the explanation as to why Aahz and I had never said anything about the house's mysterious back door. Being a seasoned dimension traveler herself, she grasped the concept of an unlisted dimension and its potential dangers much more rapidly than Guido and Nunzio.

"What I don't understand is even if he didn't want you along, why didn't he take *someone* else as a back-up?"

"Like who?" I said with a wry grimace. "We've already established that you're *my* apprentice and he doesn't give you orders without clearing them through me. He's never been impressed with Guido and Nunzio. Tananda and Chumley are off on their own contracts and aren't due back for several days. Even Gus is taking a well-earned vacation with Berfert. Besides, he knows good and well that if he started building a team and excluded me, there'd be some serious problems before the dust settled. I wouldn't take something like that lying down!"

"Don't look now, but you just did," my apprentice pointed out dryly, "though I have to admit he sort of forced it on you."

With that, she slid a hand under each of my armpits and picked me up, setting me gently on my feet.

"Well, now what? I supposed you're going to go charging after him with blood in your eye. Mind if I tag along? Or are you bound and determined to be as stupid as he is?"

As a matter of fact, that was exactly what I had been planning to do. The undisguised sarcasm in her voice combined with the unsettling wobbliness of my legs, however, led me to reconsider.

"No," I said carefully. "One of us blundering around out there is enough . . . or one too many, depending on how you count it. While I still think I should have gone along, Aahz has dealt this hand, so it's up to him to play it out. It's up to me to mind the store until he gets back."

Massha cocked an eyebrow at me.

"That makes sense," she said, "though I'll admit I'm a little surprised to hear you say it."

"I'm a responsible businessman now." I shrugged. "I can't afford to go off half-cocked like a rash kid anymore. Besides, I have every confidence in my partner's ability to handle things."

Those were brave words, and I meant them. Two days later, however, this particular 'responsible businessman' was ready to go off *fully* cocked. Guido and Nunzio ceased to complain about my sneaking off alone. . . . mostly because I didn't go out at all! In fact, I spent most of my waking hours and all of my sleeping hours (though I'll admit I didn't sleep much) in the reception room on the off-chance that I could greet Aahz on his triumphant return.

Unfortunately, my vigil went unrewarded.

I did my best to hide my concern, but I needn't have bothered. As the hours marched on, my staff's worries grew until most of my time was spent telling them, 'No, he isn't back yet. When he gets here, I'll let you know.' Even Guido, who never really got along with Aahz, took to stopping by at least once an hour for a no-progress report.

Finally, as a salve for my own nerves, I called everyone into the reception room for a staff meeting.

"What I want to know is how long are we just going to sit around before we admit that something's gone wrong?" Guido muttered for the fifth time.

"How long do you figure it takes to find a fugitive in a strange dimension?" I shot back. "How long would it take you to find them if they were on Klah, Guido? We've got to give him some time."

"How much time?" he countered. "It's already been two days. . . ."

"Tananda and Chumley will be back any time now," Massha interrupted. "Do you think they'll just sit around on their hands when they find out that Aahz is out there all alone?"

"I thought *you* were the one who thought that going after him was a stupid idea?"

"I still do. Now do you want to know what I think of the idea of doing *nothing*?"

Before I could answer, a soft knock sounded at the door...the back door!

"See!" I crowed triumphantly. "I told you he would be back!"

"That doesn't sound like his knock," Guido observed suspiciously.

"And why should he knock?" Massha added. "The door hasn't been locked since he left."

In my own relief and enthusiasm, their remarks went unnoticed. In a flash I was at the door, wrenching it open while voicing the greeting I had been rehearsing for two days.

"It's about time, part...ner."

It wasn't Aahz.

In fact, the being outside the door didn't look anything at all like Aahz. What was doubly surprising, though, was that I recognized her!

We had never really met...not to exchange names, but shortly after meeting Aahz I had been strung up by an angry mob while impersonating her, and I had seen her in the crowd when I successfully "interviewed" for the job of court magician at Possletum.

What I had never had a chance to observe first-hand was her radiant complexion framed by waves of sun-gold hair, or the easy grace with which she carried herself, or the....

"It's the Great Skeeve, right? Behind the open mouth?"

Her voice was so musical it took me a few moments to zero in on what she had said and realize that she was expecting an answer.

"Aahh...yes. I mean, at your service."

"Glad to finally meet you face-to-face," she said briskly, glancing at Guido and Massha nervously. "I've been looking for an excuse for a while, and I guess this is it. Got some news for you...about your apprentice."

I was still having problems focusing on what she was saying. Not only was her voice mesmerizing, she was easily the loveliest woman I had ever met...well, girl actually. She couldn't have been much older than me. What's more, she seemed to like me. That is, she kept smiling hesitantly and her deep blue eyes never left mine. Now, I had gotten respect from my colleagues and from beings at the Bazaar who knew my reputation, but never from anyone who looked like....

Then her words sank in.

"My apprentice?"

I stole an involuntary glance at Massha before I realized the misunderstanding.

"Oh, you mean, Aahz. He's not my apprentice any more. He's my partner. Please come in. We were just talking about him."

I stood to one side of the door and invited her in with a grand sweeping gesture. I'd never tried it before, but I had seen it used a couple of times while I was working the court at Possletum, and it had impressed me.

"Umm—Boss? Could I talk to you for a minute?"

"Later, Guido."

I repeated the gesture, and the girl responded with a quick smile that lit up the room.

"Thanks for the invite," she said, "but I'll have to take a rain check. I really can't stay. In fact, I shouldn't be here at all. I just thought that someone should let you know that your friend...Aahz is it? Anyway, your friend is in jail."

That brought me back to earth in a hurry.

"Aahz? In jail? For what?"

"Murder."

"MURDER!" I shrieked, dropping all attempts to be

urbane. "But Aahz wouldn't...."

"Don't shout at me! Oh, I knew I shouldn't have come. Look, I know he didn't do it. That's why I had to let you know what was going on. If you don't do something, they're going to execute him...and they know how to execute demons over here."

I spun around to face the others.

"Massha! Go get your jewelry case. Guido, Nunzio! Gear up. We're going to pay a little call on our neighbors."

I tried to keep my voice calm and level, but somehow the words came out a bit more intense than I had intended.

"Not so fast, Boss," Guido said. "There's something you oughta know first."

"Later. I want you to...."

"NOW, Boss. It's important!"

"WHAT IS IT!"

Needless to say, I was not eager to enter into any prolonged conversations just now.

"She's one of 'em."

"I beg your pardon?"

"The three that went out through the back door. The ones your partner is chasing. She's the broad."

Thunderstruck, I turned to the girl for confirmation, only to find the doorway was empty. My mysterious visitor had disappeared as suddenly as she had arrived.

"This could be a trap, you know," Massha said thoughtfully.

"She's right." Guido nodded. "Take it from someone who's been on the lam himself. When you're running from the law and there are only a couple of people who can find you, it gets real tempting to eliminate that link. We've only got her word that your partner's in trouble."

"It wouldn't take a mental giant to figure out that you and Aahz are the most likely hunters for the Deveels to hire. After all, they knew whose house they were cutting through for their getaway," Massha added.

Guido rose to his feet and started pacing.

"Right," he said. "Now suppose *they've* got Aahz. Can you think of a better way to bag the other half of the pair than by feeding you a line about your partner being in trouble so you'll come charging into whatever trap they've laid out? The whole set-up stinks, Boss. I don't know about strange dimensions, but I *do* know about criminals. As soon as you step through that door, you're gonna be a sitting duck."

"Are you *quite* through?"

Even to my ears my voice sounded icy, but for a change I didn't care.

Guido and Massha exchanged glances, then nodded silently.

"Very well. You may be right, and I appreciate your concern for my well-being. HOWEVER . . ."

My voice sank to a deadly hiss.

". . .what if you're wrong? What if our fugitive *is* telling the truth? You've all been on my case about not doing anything to help Aahz. Do you really think I'm just going to sit here while my partner AND friend burns for a crime he didn't commit. . .on the off-chance that getting involved *might* be dangerous to me?"

With great effort I forced my tones back to normal.

"In ten minutes I'm going through that door after Aahz. . .and if I'm walking into a trap, it had better be a good one. Now do any of you want to come with me, or am I going it alone?"

# Chapter IV

*"It's useless to try to plan for the
unexpected...by definition!"*

**A. Hitchcock**

ACTUALLY, it was more like an hour before we were
really ready to go, though for me it seemed like a lot longer.
Still, even I had to admit that not taking the proper prep-
arations for this venture would not only be foolish, it
would be downright suicidal!

It was decided that Nunzio would stay behind so
there would be someone at our base to let Tananda and
Chumley know what was going on when they returned.
Needless to say, he was less than thrilled by the
assignment.

"But I'm supposed to be your bodyguard!" he argued.
"How'm I supposed to guard you if I'm sittin' back here
while you're on the front lines?"

"By being sure our support troops get the information
they need to follow us," I said.

As much as I disliked having to argue with Nunzio, I
would rather dig in my heels against half a dozen Mob-
type bodyguards than have to explain to Tananda and
Chumley why they weren't included in this rescue
mission.

"We could leave a note."

"No."

"We could. . . ."

"NO! I want you *here*. Is that plain enough?"

The bodyguard heaved a heavy sigh. "Okay, Boss. I'll hang in here until they show up. Then the three of us will. . . ."

"No!" I said again. "Then Tananda and Chumley will come in after us. You're going to stay here."

"But Boss. . . ."

"Because if Hay-ner and his crew show up again, someone has to be here to let them know we're on the job and that we haven't just taken off for the tall timber. Assuming for the moment that we're going to make it back, we need our exit route, and you're going to be here making sure it stays open. All we need is for our hosts to move in a new tenant while we're gone. . . say, someone who decides to brick up this door while we're on the other side."

Nunzio thought this through in silence.

"What if you don't come back?" he asked finally.

"We'll burn that bridge when we come to it," I sighed. "But remember, we aren't that easy to kill. At least one of us will probably make it back."

Fortunately, my mind was wrenched away from that unpleasant train of thought by the arrival of Guido.

"Ready to go, Boss."

Despite the desperateness of the situation and the haunting time pressures, I found myself gaping at him.

"What's that?" I managed at last.

Guido was decked out in a long dark coat and wearing a wide-brimmed hat and sunglasses.

"These? These are my work clothes," he said proudly. "They're functional as well as decorative."

"They're what?"

"What I mean is, not only do people find 'em intimidating, the trench coat has all these little pockets inside, see? That's where I carry my hardware."

"But...."

"Hi, Hot Stuff. Nice outfit, Guido."

"Thanks! I was just telling the Boss here about it."

Massha was dressed...or should I say undressed in *her* work clothes. A brief vest struggled to cover even part of her massive torso, while an even briefer bottom was on the verge of surrendering its battle completely.

"Ummm...Massha?" I said carefully. "I've always meant to ask. Why don't you...ummm...wear more?"

"I like to dress cool when we're going into a hot situation," she winked. "You see, when things speed up, I get a little nervous...and the only thing worse than havin' a fat broad around is havin' a *sweaty* fat broad around."

"I think it's a sexy outfit," Guido chimed in. "Reminds me of the stuff my old man's moll used to wear."

"Well thanks, Dark and Deadly. I'd say your old man had good taste...but I never tasted him."

I studied them thoughtfully as they shared a laugh over Massha's joke. Any hope of a quiet infiltration of this unknown dimension was rapidly disintegrating. Either Guido or Massha alone was eye-catching, but together they were about as inconspicuous as a circus parade and an army maneuver sharing the same road. Then it occurred to me that, not knowing what things were like where we were heading, they might fit in and *I* would stand out. It was a frightening thought. If everybody there looked like this....

I forced the thought from my mind. No use scaring myself any more than I had to before there was information to back it up. What was important was that my two assistants were scared. They were trying hard not to show it, but in doing so, each was dropping into old patterns, slipping behind old character masks. Guido was playing his "tough gangster" bit to the hilt, while Massha was once more assuming her favorite "vamp" character with a vengeance. The bottom line, though, was that, scared or not, they were willing to back my move or die trying. It would have been touching, if it weren't for the fact that it meant they were counting on me for leadership. That meant I had to stay calm and confident...no matter how scared I felt myself. It only occurred to me as an afterthought that, in many ways, leadershp was the mask *I* was learning to slip behind when things got tight. It made me wonder briefly if *anyone* ever really knew that they were doing or felt truly confident, or if life was simply a mass game of role-playing.

"Okay. Are we ready?" I asked, shrugging off my wandering thoughts. "Massha? Got your jewelry?"

"Wearing most of it, and the rest is right here," she said, patting the pouch on her belt.

While I will occasionally make snide mental comments about my apprentice's jewelry, it serves a dual purpose. Massha's baubles are in reality a rather extensive collection of magical gimmicks she has accumulated over the years. How extensive? Well, before she signed on as my apprentice to learn real magic, she was holding down a steady job as the magician for the city-state of Ta-hoe on the dimension of Jahk solely on the strength of her collected mechanical "powers." While I agreed with Aahz that real magic was preferable to mechanical in that it was less likely to malfunction (a lesson learned from first-hand experience) I sure didn't mind having her arsenal along for back-up.

"You know that tracking ring? The one you used to find the king? Any chance there's an extra tucked away in your pouch?"

"Only have the one," she said, waggling the appropriate finger.

I cursed mentally, then made the first of what I feared would be many unpleasant decisions on this venture.

"Give it to Nunzio. Tananda and Chumley will need it to find us."

"But if we leave it behind, how are we going to find your partner?"

"We'll have to figure out something, but we can't afford to divide our forces. Otherwise, even if we get Aahz, we could still end up wandering around out there trying to find the other half of the rescue team."

"If you say so, Hot Stuff," she grimaced, handing over the ring, "but I hope you know what you're doing."

"So do I, Massha, so do I. Okay, gang, let's see what our backyard is *really* like!"


FROM the outside, our place looked a lot more impressive than the side that showed in the Bazaar. It really did look like a castle...a rather ominous one at that, squatting alone on a hilltop. I really didn't study it too close, though, beyond being able to recognize it again for our trip out. As might be expected, my main attention was focused on the new dimension itself.

"Kinda dark, ain't it."

Guido's comment was more statement than question, and he was right.

Wherever we were, the lighting left a lot to be desired. At first I thought it was night, which puzzled me, as so far in my travels all dimensions seemed to be on the same sun-up and sun-down schedule. Then my eyes adjusted to the gloom and I realized the sky was simply heavily overcast...to a point where next to no light at all penetrated, giving a night-like illusion to the day.

Aside from that, from what I could see, this new land seemed pretty much like any of the others I had visited: Trees, underbrush, and a road leading to or from the castle, depending on which way you were facing. I think it was Tananda who was fond of saying "If you've seen one dimension, you've seen them all." Chumley, her brother, argued that the reason for the geologic similarities was that all the dimensions we traveled were different realities off the same base. This always struck me as being a bit redundant... "They're all alike because they're the same? C'mon Chumley!", but his rebuttals always left me feeling like I'd been listening to someone doing readings in another language, so of late I've been tending to avoid the discussions.

"Well, Hot Stuff, what do we do now?"

For a change, I had an answer for this infuriating question.

"This road has to go somewhere. Just the fact that it exists indicates we aren't alone in this dimension."

"I thought we already knew that," Guido said under his breath. "That's why we're here."

I gave him my best dark glare.

"I believe there was *some* debate as to whether or not we were being lied to about Aahz being held prisoner. If there's a road here, it's a cinch that neither my partner nor the ones he was chasing built it. That means we have native types to deal with...possibly hostile."

"Right," Massha put in quickly. "Put a sock in it, Guido. I want to hear our plan of action, and I don't like being kept waiting by hecklers."

The bodyguard frowned, but kept his silence.

"Okay. Now, what we've got to do is follow this road and find out where it goes. Hug the side of the road and be ready to disappear if you hear anybody coming. We don't know what the locals look like, and until I have a model to work from, it's pointless for me to try to disguise us."

With those general marching orders, we made our way through the dark along the road, moving quietly to avoid tipping our hand to anyone ahead of us. In a short time we came up to our first decision point. The road we were on ended abruptly when it met another, much larger thoroughfare. My assistants looked at me expectantly. With a shrug I made the arbitrary decision and led them off to the right down this new course. As we went, I reflected with some annoyance that even though both

Massha and Guido knew that I was as new to this terrain as they were, it somehow fell to me to choose the path.

My thoughts were interrupted by the sound of voices ahead, coming our way. The others heard it too, and without word or signal we melted into the underbrush. Squatting down, I peered through the gloom toward the road, anxious to catch my first glimpse of the native life forms.

I didn't have long to wait. Two figures appeared, a young couple by the look of them, talking and laughing merrily as they went. They looked pretty normal to me, which was a distinct relief, considering the forms I had had to imitate in some of the other dimensions. They were humanoid enough to pass for Klahds . . . or Jahks, actually, as they were a bit pale. Their dress was not dissimilar from my own, though a bit more colorful. Absorbing all this in a glance, I decided to make my first try for information. I mean, after all my fears, they were so familiar it was almost a letdown, so why not bull ahead? Compared with some of the beings I've had to deal with in the past, this looked like a piece of cake.

Signaling the others to stay put, I stepped out onto the road behind my target couple.

"Excuse me!" I called "I'm new to this area and in need of a little assistance. Could you direct me to the nearest town?"

Translation pendants were standard equipment for dimension travel, and as I was wearing one now, I had no fear of not being understood.

The couple turned to face me, and I was immediately struck by their eyes. The "whites" of their eyes glowed a dark red, sending chills down my spine. It occurred to me that I might have studied the locals a bit longer before I tried to pass myself off as a native. It also occurred to me that I had already committed myself to this course of action and would have to bluff my way through it regardless. Finally, it occurred to me that I was a suicidal idiot and that I hoped Massha and Guido were readying their back-up weapons to save me from my own impatience.

Strangely enough, the couple didn't seem to notice anything unusual about my appearance.

"The nearest town? That would be Blut. It's not far, we just came from there. It's got a pretty wild night life, if you're into that kind of thing."

There was something about his mouth that nagged at the edges of my mind. Unfortunately, I couldn't look at it directly without breaking eye contact, so, buoyed by my apparent acceptance, I pushed ahead with the conversation.

"Actually, I'm not too big on night life. I'm trying to run down an old friend of mine I've lost touch with. Is there a post office or a police station in Blut I could ask at?"

"Better than that," the man laughed. "The one you want to talk to is the Dispatcher. He keeps tabs on every-body. The third warehouse on your left as you enter town. He's converted the whole second floor into an office. If he can't help you, nobody can."

As vital as the information was, I only paid it partial attention. When the man laughed, I had gotten a better look at his mouth. His teeth were. . . .

"Look at his teeth!" the girl gasped, speaking for the first time.

"My teeth?" I blinked, realizing with a start that she was staring at me with undisguised astonishment.

Her companion, in the meantime, had paled notice-ably and was backing away on unsteady legs.

"You. . .you're. . .Where did you come from?"

Trying my best to maintain a normal manner until I had figured out what was going on, I moved forward to keep our earlier conversational distance.

"The castle on the hill back there. I was just. . . ."

"THE CASTLE!?!"

In a flash the couple turned and sprinted away from

35

me down the road.

"Monster!! Help!! MONSTER!!!"

I actually spun and looked down the road behind me, trying to spot the object of their terror. Looking at the empty road, however, it slowly began to sink in. They were afraid of *me*! Monster?

Of all the reactions I had tried to anticipate for our reception in this new land, I had never in my wildest imaginings expected this.

Me? A monster?

"I think we've got problems, High Roller," Massha said as she and Guido emerged from the brush at my side.

"I'll say. Unless I'm reading the signs all wrong, they're afraid of me."

She heaved a great sigh and shook her head.

"That's not what I'm talking about. Did you see their teeth?"

"I saw his," I said. "The canines were long and pointed. Pretty weird, huh?"

"Not all that weird, Hot Stuff. Think about it. My bet is that you were just talking to a couple of vampires!"

# Chapter V

*"To survive, one must be able to adapt to changing situations."*
**Tyrannosaurus Rex**

V AMPIRES," I said carefully.

"Sure. It all fits." Massha nodded. "The pale skin, the sharp fangs, the red eyeliner, the way they turned into bats...."

"Turned into bats?"

"You missed it, Boss," Guido supplied. "You were lookin' behind you when they did it. Wildest thing I ever saw. One second they was runnin' for their lives, and the next they're flutterin' up into the dark. Are all the other dimensions like this?"

"Vampires...."

Actually, my shock wasn't all that great. Realizing the things Aahz and I had run into cruising the so-called "known and safe" dimensions, I had expected something a bit out of the ordinary in this one. If anything, I was a bit relieved. The second shoe had been dropped...and it really wasn't all that bad! That is, it could have been worse. (If hanging around with Aahz had taught me any-thing, it was that things could always be worse!) The repetitive nature of my conversational brilliance was merely a clever ploy to cover my mental efforts to both digest this new bit of information and decide what to do with it.

"Vampires are rare in any dimension," my apprentice replied, stepping into the void to answer Guido's question. "What's more, they're pretty much feared universally. What I can't figure out is why those two were so scared of Skeeve here."

"Then again," I said thoughtfully, "there's the question of whether or not we can safely assume the whole dimension is populated with beings like the two we just met. I know it's a long shot, but we might have run into the only two vampires in the place."

"I dunno, High Roller. They acted pretty much at home here, and they sure didn't think you'd find anything unusual about *their* appearance. My guess is that they're the norm and we're the exceptions around here."

"Whatever," I said, reaching a decision at last, "they're the only two examples we have to work with so far, so that's what we'll base our actions on until proven different."

"So what do we do against a bunch of vampires?"

As a bodyguard, Guido seemed a bit uneasy about our assessment of the situation.

"Relax," I smiled. "The first order of business is to turn on the old reliable disguise spell. Just a few quick touch-ups and they won't be able to tell us apart from the natives. We could walk through a town of vampires and they'd never spot us."

With that, I closed my eyes and went to work. Like I told the staff, this was going to be easy. Maintain everyone's normal appearance except for paler skin, longer canines, and a little artful reddening of the eyes, and the job was done.

"Okay," I said, opening my eyes again. "What's next?"

"I don't like to quote you back at yourself, Hot Stuff,"

Massha drawled, "but didn't you say something about disguises being the first thing before we went any further?"

"Of course. That's why I just...wait a minute. Are you trying to say we still have the same appearance as before I cast the spell?"

One of the problems with casting a disguise spell is that as the caster, I can never see the effects. That is, I see people as they really are whether the spell is on or not. I had gotten so used to relying on the effects of this particular spell that it had never occurred to me that it might not work.

Massha and Guido were looking at each other with no small degree of concern.

"Ummm...maybe you forgot."

"Try again."

"That's right! This time remember to...."

"Hold it, you two," I ordered in my most commanding tone. "From your reactions, I perceive that the answer to my questions is 'yes.' That is, that the spell didn't work. Now just ease up a second and let me think. Okay?"

For a change they listened to me and lapsed into a respectful silence. I might have taken a moment to savor the triumph if I wasn't so worried about the problem.

The disguise spell was one of the first spells I had learned, and until now was one of my best and most reliable tools. If it wasn't working, something was seriously wrong. Now I knew that stepping through the door hadn't lessened my knowledge of that particular spell, so that meant that if something was haywire, it would have to be in the....

"Hey, Hot Stuff! Check the force lines!"

Apparently my apprentice and I had reached the conclusion simultaneously. A quick magical scan of the sky overhead and the surrounding terrain confirmed my worst fears. At first I thought there were no force lines at all. Then I realized that they were there, but so faint that it took nearly all of my reserve power just to detect them.

"What's all this about force lines?" Guido demanded.

Massha heaved an impatient sigh.

"If you're going to run with this crowd, Dark and Deadly, you'd best start learning a little about the magic biz...or at least the vocabulary. Force lines are invisible streams of energy that flow through the ground and the air. They're the source of power we tap into when we do our bibbity-bobbity-boo schtick. That means that in a land like this one, where the force lines are either non-existent or very weak...."

"...you can't do squat," the bodyguard finished for her. "Hey, Boss! If what she says is true, how come those two you just met could still do that bat-trick?"

"By being very, *very* good in the magic department. To do so much with so little means they don't miss a trick...pardon the pun...in tapping and using force lines. In short, they're a lot better than either Massha or me at the magic game."

"That makes sense." Massha nodded. "In any dimension I've been in that had vampires, they were some of the strongest magic-slingers around. If this is what they have to train on, I can see why they run hog-wild when they hit a dimension where the force lines are both plentiful and powerful."

I rubbed my forehead, trying desperately to think and to forestall the headache I felt coming on. Right on schedule, things were getting worse!

"I don't suppose you have anything in your jewelry collection that can handle disguises, do you?"

Despite our predicament, Massha gave a low laugh.

"Think about it, High Roller. If I had anything that could do disguises, would I walk around looking like this?"

"So we get to take on a world of hot-shot magic types with our own cover fire on low ammo," Guido summarized.

"Okay. So it'll be a little tougher than I thought at

first. Just remember my partner has been getting along pretty well these last few years without any powers at all."

"Your partner is currently sitting in the hoosegow for murder," Guido said pointedly. "That's why we're here in the first place. Remember?"

"Besides," I continued, ignoring his comment (that's another skill I've learned from Aahz), "it's never been our intention 'to take on the whole world.' All we want to do is perform a quick hit and run. Grab Aahz and get back out with as little contact with the natives as possible. All this means is that we've got to be a little more careful. That's all."

"What about running down the trio we started out to retrieve?"

I thought briefly about the blonde who had warned us of Aahz's predicament.

"That's part of being more careful," I announced solemnly. "If. . . I mean, *when* we get Aahz out of jail, we'll head for home and count ourselves as lucky. So we. . . pay off the Deveels. It's a. . . cheap price to. . . pay for. . . ."

I realized the staff was looking at me a little askance. I also realized that my words had been gradually slowing to a painful broken delivery as I reached the part about paying off the Deveels.

I cleared my throat and tried again.

"Ummm, let's just say we'll reappraise the situation once we've reached Aahz. Okay?"

The troops still looked a little dubious, so I thought it would be best if I pushed on to the next subject.

"As to the opposition, let's pool our knowledge of vampires so we have an idea of what we're up against. Now, we know they can shapechange into bats or dogs. . . ."

". . . or just into a cloud of mist," Massha supplied.

"They drink blood," Guido said grimly.

"They don't like bright light, or crosses. . . ."

"...and they can be killed by a stake through their heart or...."

"They drink blood."

"Enough with the drinking blood! Okay, Guido?"

I was starting to get more than a little annoyed with my bodyguard's endless pessimism. I mean, none of us was particularly pleased by the way things were going, but there was nothing to be gained by dwelling on the negatives.

"Sorry, Boss. I guess looking on the dark side of things gets to be a habit in my business."

"Garlic!" Massha exclaimed suddenly.

"What's that?"

"I said 'garlic'," she repeated. "Vampires don't like garlic!"

"That's right! How about it, Guido? Do you have any garlic along?"

The bodyguard actually looked embarrassed.

"Can't stand the stuff," he admitted "The other boys in the Mob used to razz me about it, but it makes me break out in a rash."

Terrific. We probably had the only Mob member in existence who was allergic to garlic. Another brilliant idea shot to hell.

"Well," I said, heaving a sigh, "now we know what we're up against."

"Ummm...say, Hot Stuff?" Massha said softly. "All kidding aside. Aren't we a little overmatched on this one? I mean, Dark and Deadly here can hold up his end on the physical protection side, but I'm not sure my jewelry collection is going to be enough to cover us magically."

"I appreciate the vote of confidence," Guido smiled sadly, "but I'm not sure my hardware is going to do us a lick of good against vampires. With the Boss out of action on the magic side...."

"Don't count me out so fast. My magic may not be at full power, but I can still pull off a trick or two if things really get rough."

Massha frowned. "But the force lines...."

"There's one little item I've omitted from your lessons so far, apprentice," I said with a smug little grin. "It hasn't really been necessary what with the energy so plentiful on Deva...as a matter of fact, I've kind of gotten out of the habit myself. Anyway, what it boils down to is that you don't always tap into a force line to work magic. You can store the energy internally like a battery so that it's there when you need it. While we've been talking, I've been charging up, so I can provide a bit of magical cover as needed. Now, I won't be able to do anything prolonged like a constant disguise spell, and what I've got I'll want to use carefully because it'll take a while to recharge after each use, but we won't be relying on your jewelry completely."

I had expected a certain amount of excitement from the staff when they found out I wasn't totally helpless. Instead, they looked uncomfortable. They exchanged glances, then looked at the sky, then at the ground.

"Ummm...does this mean we're going on?" Guido said at last.

"That's right," I said, lips tight. "In fact, I probably would have gone on even if my powers were completely gone. Somewhere out there my partner's in trouble, and I'm not going to back away from at least *trying* to help him. I'd do the same if it was one of you, but we're talking about Aahz here. He's saved my skin more times than I care to remember. I can't just...."

I caught myself and brought my voice back under control.

"Look," I said, starting again. "I'll admit we never expected this vampire thing when we started out, and the limited magic handicap is enough to give anyone pause. If either or both of you want to head back, you can do it without hard feelings or guilt trips. Really. The only reason I'm pushing on is that I know me. Whatever is up ahead, it can't be any worse than what I would put myself through if I left Aahz alone to die without trying my best to bail him out. But that's me. If you want out, go ahead."

"Don't get your back up, Hot Stuff," Massha chided gently. "I'm still not sure how much help I'm going to be, but I'll tag along. I'd probably have the same problem if anything happened to you and I wasn't there, that you'd have if anything happened to Aahz. I *am* your apprentice, you know."

"Bodyguarding ain't much, but it's all I know," Guido said glumly. "I'm supposed to be guardin' that body of yours, so where it goes, I go. I'm just not wild about the odds, know what I mean?"

"Then it's settled," I said firmly. "All right. As I see it, our next stop is Blut."

"Blut," Massha echoed carefully.

"That's right. I want to look up this Dispatcher character and see what he has to say. I mean, a town is a town, and we've all visited strange towns before. What we really need now is information, and the nearest source seems to be Blut."

"The Dispatcher," Massha said without enthusiasm."

"Blut," Guido repeated with even less joyful anticipation.

It occurred to me that while my assistants were bound and determined to stay with me on this caper, if I wanted wholehearted support, I'd better look for it from the natives...a prospect I didn't put much hope in at all.

# Chapter VI

*"An agent is a vampire
with a telephone!"*

**any editor**

REMEMBER how I said that if you've seen one town, you've seen 'em all? Well, forget it. Even though I've visited a lot of dimensions and seen a lot of towns, I had to admit that Blut looked a little strange.

Everything seemed to be done to death in basic black. (Perhaps "done to death" is an unfortunate turn of a phrase. Whatever.) Mind you, when I say everything, I mean *everything.* Cobblestones, walls, roof tiles, everything had the same uninspired color scheme. Maybe by itself the black overtones wouldn't have seemed too ominous, if it weren't for the architectural decorations that seemed to abound everywhere you looked. Stone dragons and snakes adorned every roof peak and ledge, along with the inescapable gargoyles and, of course, bats. I don't mean "bats" here, I mean "BATS"!!! Big bats, little bats, bats with their wings half open and others with their wings spread wide...BATS!!! The only thing they all seemed to have in common (besides being black) was mouths full of needle-sharp teeth...an image which did nothing to further the confidence of my already nervous party. I myself felt the tension increasing as we strode down the street under the noses of those fierce adornments. One almost expected the stone figures to come to life and swoop down on us for a pint or two of dinner.

"Cheerful sort of place, isn't it?" Massha asked, eyeing the rooftops.

"I don't like to complain, Boss," Guido put in, lying blatantly, "but I've been in friendlier-looking graveyards."

"Will you both keep your mouths shut!" I snarled, speaking as best I could through tightly pressed lips. "Remember our disguises."

I had indeed turned on my disguise spell as we entered town, but in an effort to conserve magical energy, I had only turned our eyes red. If any of the others on the street, and there were lots of them, happened to spot our non-vampirish teeth, the balloon would go up once and for all. Then again, maybe not. We still hadn't figured out why the couple we met on the road had been so afraid of me, but I wasn't about to bank the success of our mission on anything as flimsy as a hope that the whole town would run at the sight of our undisguised features.

Fortunately, I didn't have to do any magical tinkering with our wardrobe. If anything, we were a little drab compared to most of the vampires on the street. Though most of them appeared rather young, barely older than me, they came in all shapes and sizes, and were decked out in some of the most colorful and outrageous garb it has ever been my misfortune to encounter as they shouted to each other or wove their way in and out of taverns along the street.

It was night now, the clouds having cleared enough to show a star-studded night sky, and true to their billing, vampires seemed to love the night life.

"If everybody here is vampires," Guido said, ignoring my warning, "how do they find anybody to bite for blood?"

"As far as I can tell," Massha answered, also choosing to overlook the gag order, "they buy it by the bottle."

She pointed to a small group of vampires sitting on a low wall merrily passing a bottle of red liquid back and forth among themselves. Despite our knowledge of the area, I had subconsciously assumed they were drinking wine. Confronted by the inescapable logic that the stuff they were drinking was typed, not aged, my stomach did a fast roll and dip to the right.

"If you two are through sightseeing," I hissed, "let's try to find this Dispatcher character before someone invites us to join them for a drink."

With that, I led off my slightly subdued assistants, nodding and waving at the merrymaking vampires as we went. Actually, the goings on looked like a lot of fun, and I might have been tempted to join in, if it weren't for the urgency of our quest...and, of course, the fact that they *were* vampires.

Following the instructions I had gleaned from the couple on the road before their panicky flight, we found the Dispatcher's place with no problem. Leaving Guido outside as a lookout, Massha and I braved the stairs and entered the Dispatcher's office.

As strange as Blut had appeared, it hadn't prepared me for the room we stepped into.

There were hundreds of glass pictures lining the walls, pictures which depicted moving, living things much like looking into a rack of fishbowls. What was more, the images being displayed were of incredible violence and unspeakable acts being performed in seemingly helpless victims. The overall effect was neither relaxing nor pleasant...definitely not something I'd want on the wall at home.

I was so entranced by the pictures, I almost missed the Dispatcher himself until he rose from his desk. Perhaps "rose" is the wrong description. What he actually did was hop down to the floor from his chair which was high to begin with, but made higher by the addition of a pillow to the seat.

He strode forward, beaming widely, with his hand extended for a handshake.

"Hi there Vilhelm's the name Your problem is my problem Don't sit down Standing problems I solve for free Sitting problems I charge for Reasonable rates Just a minor percentage off the top What can I do for you?"

That was sort of all one sentence in that he didn't pause for breath. He did, however, seize my hand, pump it twice, then repeated the same procedure with Massha, then grabbed my hand again...all before he stopped talking.

All in all, it was a little overpowering. I had a flash impression of a short, stocky character with plump rosy cheeks and a bad case of the fidgets. I had deliberately tried not to speculate on what the Dispatcher would look like, but a cherub vampire still caught me a little off-guard.

"I...ummm...how did you know I have a problem?"

That earned me an extra squeeze of the hand and a wink.

"Nobody comes in here unless they've got a problem," he said, finally slowing down his speech a bit. "I mean, I could always use a bit of help, but does anyone leap forward to lend a hand? Fat chance. Seems like the only time I see another face in the flesh is when it means more work for me. Prove me wrong...please! Tell me you came in here to take over for an hour or so to let me duck out for a bite to drink."

"Well, actually, we've got a problem and we were told...."

"See! What did I tell you? All right. What have you got? A standing or a sitting problem? Standing problems I handle for...."

He was off again. In a desperate effort to keep our visit short, I interrupted his pitch.

"We're looking for a friend who...."

"Say no more! A friend! Just a second!"

With that he vaulted back into his chair, grabbed the

top off a strange-looking appliance on his desk, diddled with it briefly, then started talking into it.

"Yea Darwin? Vilhelm. I need...sure...."

Leaning back in his chair, he tucked the gadget under one side of his head and grabbed another.

"This is Vilhelm. Is Kay around?...Well, put her on when she's done...."

The second gadget slid in under the same ear as the first and he reached for yet another.

"I know I shouldn't ask this," I murmured to Massha, "but what's he doing?"

"Those are telephones," she whispered back as a fourth instrument came into play. "You talk into one end of it and whoever's at the other end can hear you and talk back. It beats running all over town to find an answer."

By this time, the little vampire had so many instruments hung from his shoulders and arms he looked like he was being attacked by a nest of snakes. He seemed to be handling it well, though, talking first into one, then another, apparently keeping multiple conversations going at once like a juggler handles a basket full of balls.

"Gee, that's kind of neat!" I exclaimed. "Do you think we could get some of these for our place at the Bazaar?"

"Believe me, they're more trouble than they're worth," Massha said. "In nothing flat you find you're spending all your time on the phone talking to people and not accomplishing anything. Besides, ever since they broke up the corporation...."

"I think I've got it!" Vilhelm announced, jumping down to floor-level again. "I've got one friend for you definite, but to be honest with you he's only so-so. I've got call-backs coming on two others, so let's see what they're like before you commit on the definite. Okay?"

"Ummm...I think there's some kind of mistake here," I said desperately, trying to stop the madness before it progressed any further. "I'm not trying to find a *new* friend. I'm trying to locate a friend I already have who

49

may be here in town."

He blinked several times as this news sank in. He started to turn back to his phones in an involuntary motion, then waved a hand at them in disgusted dismissal.

"Heck with it," he said with a sigh. "If they can come up with anything, I can always fob 'em off on someone else for a profit. Now then, let's try this again. You're looking for someone specific. Are they are a townie or a transient? It *would* help if you gave me a little something to go on, you know."

He seemed a little annoyed, and I would have liked to do or say something to cheer him up. Before I could think of anything, however, my apprentice decided to join the conversation.

"This is quite a layout you've got, Fast Worker. Mind if I ask exactly what it is you do?"

As always, Massha's "people sense" proved to be better than mine. The little vampire brightened noticeably at the compliment, and his chest puffed out as he launched into his narration.

"Well, the job was originally billed as Dispatcher... you know, as in Dispatcher of Nightmares. But anyway, like any job, it turned out to involve a lot of things that aren't on the job description. Now it's sort of a combination of dispatcher, travel agent, lost and found, and missing persons bureau."

"Nightmares?" I questioned, unable to contain myself.

"Sure. Anything that comes out of Limbo, be it dreams or the real thing, comes through here. Where're you from that you didn't know that?"

Obviously, I wasn't wild about continuing on the subject of our place of origin.

"Ahhh, can you really help us find our friend? He's new in town, like us."

"That's right. You're looking for someone. Sorry. I get a little carried away sometimes when I talk about my

50

work. New in town, hmmm? Shouldn't be that hard to locate. We don't get that many visitors."

"He might be in jail," Massha blurted out before I realized what she was going to say.

"In jail?" The vampire frowned. "The only outsider in jail right now is. . . . Say! Now I recognize you! The eyes threw me for a minute. You're Skeeve, aren't you?"

"Screen 97B!" he declared proudly, gesturing vaguely over his shoulder. "There's someone a dozen dimensions over from here, runs a hot dog stand, who features you in his most frequent nightmares. You, a dragon, and a Pervert. Am I correct in assuming that the current resident in our fair jail is none other than your sidekick Aahz?"

"To be correct, that's Pervect, not Pervert...but except for that you're right. That's my partner you've got locked up there, and we aim to get him out."

I was probably talking too much, but being recognized in a dimension I'd never heard of had thrown me off balance. Then again, the Dispatcher didn't seem all that hostile at the discovery. More curious than anything else.

"Well, well. Skeeve himself. I never expected to meet you in person. Sometime you must tell me what you did to that poor fellow to rate the number-one slot on his hit parade of nightmares."

"What about Aahz?" I said impatiently.,

"You know he's up for murder, don't you?"

"Heard it. Don't believe it. He's a lot of things, but a murderer isn't one of them."

"There's a fair amount of evidence." Vilhelm shrugged. "But tell me. What's with the vampire get-up. You're no more a vampire than I'm a Klahd."

"It's a long story. Let's just say it seemed to be the local uniform."

"Let's not," the dispatcher grinned. "Pull up a

chair...free of charge, of course. I've got time and lots of questions about the other dimensions. Maybe we can trade a little information while you're here."

# Chapter VII

### *"I don't see anything thrilling about it!"*
### M. Jackson

I really don't see how you can drink that stuff," I declared, eyeing Vilhelm's goblet of blood.

"Funny," he smiled in return, "I was about to say the same thing. I mean, you know what W. C. Fields said about water!"

"No, What?"

"Now let me get this straight," Guido interrupted before I could get any answer. "You're sayin' you vampire guys don't really drink blood from people?"

"Oh, a few do," the Dispatcher said with a shrug. "But it's an acquired taste, like steak tartare. Some say it's a gourmet dish, but I could never stand the stuff myself. I'll stick with the inexpensive domestic varieties any night."

We were all sprawled around the Dispatcher's office at this point, sipping our respective drinks and getting into a pretty good rap session. We had pulled Guido in off door watch and I had dropped our disguises so my energy reserve wasn't being drained."

The Dispatcher had played with his phones, calling

from one to the other. Then he put them all down and announced that he had them on "hold," a curious expression since it was the first time in half an hour he hadn't been holding one.

Vilhelm himself was turning out to be a priceless source of information, and, as promised, had a seemingly insatiable curiosity about otherworldly things.

"Then how do you account for all the vampire legends around the other dimensions," Massha said skeptically.

The Dispatcher made a face.

"First of all, you've got to realize who you're dealing with. Most of the ones who do extensive touring outside of Limbo are 'old money' types. We're talking about the idle rich...and that usually equates to bored thrillseekers. Working stiffs like me can't afford to take that kind of time away from our jobs. Heck, I can hardly manage to get my two weeks each year. Anyway, there are a lot more of us around the dimensions than you might realize. It's just that the level-headed ones are content to maintain a low profile and blend with the natives. They content themselves with the blood of domestic livestock, much the way we do here at home. It's the others that cause the problems. Like any group of tourists, there's always a few who feel that just because they're in another world or city, the rules don't apply...and that includes common manners and good taste. They're the ones who stir up trouble by getting the locals up in arms about 'bloodsucking monsters.' If it makes you feel any better, you human types have a pretty bad rep yourselves here in Limbo."

That caught my attention.

"Could you elaborate on that last point, Vilhelm? What problem could the locals have with us?"

The Dispatcher laughed.

"The same one you humans have with us vampires. While humans aren't the leading cause of death in vampires any more than vampires are a leading cause of death in humans, it's certainly one of the more publicized and sensational ways to go."

"Is that why the first locals we met took off like bats out of hell...if you'll pardon the expression?" Massha asked.

"You've got it. I think you'll find that the citizens of Blut will react the same way to you that you would if you ran into a vampire in your home dimension."

"I don't notice you bein' particularly scared of us," Guido said suspiciously.

"One of the few advantages of this job. After a few years of monitoring the other dimensions, you get pretty blasé about demons. As far as I can tell, most of 'em are no worse than some of the folks we've got around here."

This was all very interesting, but I was getting a little fidgety about our mission.

"Since you know we aren't all evil or on a permanent vampire hunt, what can you tell us about the mess Aahz is in? Can you give us any help there?"

"I dunno," the Dispatcher said, rubbing his jaw thoughtfully. "Until I found out who he was, I was ready to believe he was guilty as sin. There's an awful lot of evidence against him."

"Such as?" I pressed.

"Well, he was caught with a stake and mallet in his hand, and there are two eyewitnesses who say they saw him kill one of our citizens and scatter his dust to the winds."

"Wait a minute. You mean you ain't got no *corpus delecti*?" Guido said, straightening in his chair. "Sorry to interrupt, Boss, but you're playin' in my alley now. This is somethin' I know a little about. You can't go on trial for murder without a corpse, know what I mean?"

"Maybe where you come from," Vilhelm corrected, "but things get a little different when you're dealing with vampires. If we *had* a body, or even just the pile of dust, we could revive him in no time flat. As it is, the problem is when there's *no* body...when a vampire's been reduced to dust and the dust scattered. That's when it's impossible to pull 'em back into a functional mode."

"But if there isn't a body, how do you know the victim is dead at all?" I asked.

"There's the rub," Vilhelm agreed. "But in this case, there's a matter of two eyewitnesses."

"Two of 'em, eh?" Massha murmured thoughtfully. "Would you happen to have descriptions of these two peepers?"

"Saw 'em myself. They were both off-worlders like yourselves. One was a young girl, the blonde and innocent type. The other was a pretty sleazy-looking guy. It was her who sold us on the story, really. I don't think anyone would have believed him if he said that werewolves were furry."

My heart sank. I had wanted very badly to believe the girl who had warned us of Aahz's danger was somehow an innocent bystander in the proceedings. Now it looked as if....

"Do the descriptions sound familiar, Hot Stuff? Still think Guido and I were being paranoid when we said this might be a set-up? Sounds like they framed your partner, then came back after you to complete the set."

I avoided her eyes, staring hard at the wall monitors.

"There might be another explanation, you know."

My apprentice gave out a bark of laughter.

"If there is, I'm dying to hear it. Face it, High Roller, any way you look at it the situation stinks. If they cooked up a frame that tight on Green and Scaly on such short notice, I'm dying to see what kind of a trap they've got waiting for you now that they've had time to get ready *before* inviting you to step in."

It occurred to me that I had never been that mouthy when I was an apprentice. It also occurred to me that now I understood why Aahz had gotten so angry on the rare occasions when I had voiced an opinion...and the rarer times when I was right.

"I think I missed a lap in this conversation some-where." Vilhelm frowned. "I take it you know the witnesses?"

Massha proceeded to bring the Dispatcher up to date, with Guido growling counterpoint to the theme. For once I was glad to let them do the talking. It gave me a chance to collect my scattered thoughts and try to formulate a plan. When they finished, I still had a long way to go on both counts.

"I must admit, viewed from the light of this new information, the whole thing does sound a little suspicious," the vampire said thoughtfully.

"A *little* suspicious!" Massha snorted. "It's phonier than a smiling Deveel!"

"Tell ya what," Guido began, "just give us a few minutes alone with these witnesses of yours and we'll shake the truth out of 'em."

"I'm afraid that will be a little difficult," the Dispatcher said, eyeing the ceiling. "You see, they haven't been around for a while. Disappeared right after the trial."

"The trial!?" I snapped, abandoning my efforts to collect my wits. "You mean the trial's already been held?"

The vampire nodded.

"That's right. Needless to say, your friend was found guilty."

"Why do I get the feeling he didn't get a suspended sentence for a first offense?" Guido growled under his breath.

"As a matter of fact, he's been slated for execution at the end of the week," Vilhelm admitted.

That got me out of my seat and pacing.

"We've got to do something," I said needlessly. "How about it, Vilhelm? Can you help us out at all? Any chance of getting the verdict reversed or at least a stay of execution?"

"I'm afraid not. Character witnesses alone wouldn't change anything, and as for new evidence, it would only be your word against the existing witnesses...and you've already admitted the defendant is a friend of yours. Mind you, *I* believe you, but there are those who would suspect you'd say anything or fabricate any kind of tale to save your partner."

"But can you *personally* give us a hand?"

"No, I can't," the vampire said, turning away. "You all seem like real nice folks, and your friend is probably the salt of the earth, but I have to live here and deal with these people for a long time. If I sided with outsiders against the town legal system, my whole career would go down the drain whether I was right or not. It's not pretty and I don't like it, but that's the way things are."

"We could fix it so you like it a lot less!" Guido said darkly, reaching into his coat.

"Stop it, Guido," I ordered. "Let's not forget the help Vilhelm's *already* given us. It's a lot more than we expected to get when we first came into this dimension, so don't go making enemies out of the only friend we've got locally. Okay?"

The bodyguard sank back into his chair, muttering something I was just as glad I didn't hear, but his hand came out of his coat empty and stayed in sight.

"So what do we do now, Hot Stuff?" Massha sighed.

"The only thing I can think of is to try to locate those witnesses before the execution date," I said. "What I can't figure is how to go about looking without getting half the town down on our necks."

"What we really need is a bloodhound," Guido grumbled.

"Say, that's not a bad idea!" Vilhelm exclaimed, coming to life. "Maybe I can help you after all!"

"You got a bloodhound?" the bodyguard said, raising his eyebrows.

"Even better," the vampire declared. "I don't know

why I didn't think of it before. The ones you need to get in touch with are the Woof Writers."

I studied him carefully to see if this were some kind of joke.

"The Woof Writers?" I repeated at last.

"Well, that's what we in Blut call them behind their backs. Actually, they're a husband-wife team of were-wolves who are on a big crusade to raise sympathy for humans."

"Werewolves," I said carefully.

"Sure. We got all kinds here in Limbo. Anyway, if anyone in this dimension will be willing to stick their necks out for you, they're the ones. They do their own thing and don't really give a hang what any of the other locals think about it. Besides, werewolves are second to none when it comes to sniffing out a trail."

"Werewolves."

Vilhelm cocked his head at me curiously.

"Am I imagining things, Skeeve, or didn't you just say that?"

"What's more," Massha smiled sweetly, "he'll probably say it again. It bears repeating."

"Werewolves," I said again, just to support my apprentice.

"Boss," Guido began, "I don't want to say this, but nobody said anything about werewolves when we...."

"Good," I interrupted brusquely. "You don't want to say it, and I don't want to hear it. Now that we're in agreement, let's just pass on it and...."

"But Boss! We can't team up with werewolves."

"Guido, we just went over this. We're in a tight spot *and* in a strange dimension. We can't afford to be choosy about our allies."

"You don't understand, Boss. I'm allergic to 'em!"

I sank down into a chair and hid my face in my hands.

"I thought you were allergic to garlic," I said through my fingers.

"That, too," the bodyguard said. "But mostly I'm allergic to furry things like kitties or fur coats or...."

"...or werewolves," Massha finished for him. "Frankly, Dark and Deadly, one starts to wonder how you've been able to function effectively all these years."

"Hey, it doesn't come up all that often, know what I mean?" Guido argued defensively. "How many times have *you* been attacked by somethin' furry?"

"Not as often as I'd like!" Massha leered.

"Enough, you two," I ordered, raising my head. "Guido, have you ever actually been near a werewolf?"

"Well, no. But...."

"Then until we know for sure, we'll assume you're *not* allergic to them. Okay? Vilhelm, exactly where do we find these Woof Writers of yours?"

# Chapter VIII

*"First, let's decide who's leading
and who's following."*
F. Astaire

BOSS, just where the hell *is* Pahkipsee?"

I found myself wondering if all bodyguards spent most of their time complaining, or if I had just gotten lucky.

"Look, Guido. You were there and heard the same instructions I did. If Vilhelm was right, it should be just up the road here a couple more miles."

"... 'a rather dead bedroom community, fit only for those not up to the fast-lane life-style of the big city,'" Massha quoted in a close imitation of the vampire's voice.

Guido snickered rudely.

"Why do I get the feeling you didn't particularly warm to Vilhelm, Massha?" I suppressed a grin of my own.

"Maybe it's because he's the only guy we've met she hasn't made a pass at?" Guido suggested.

Massha favored him with an extended tongue and crossed eyes before answering.

"Oh, Vilhelm's okay," she said. "Kinda cute, too...at least the top of his head was. And he did admit that in general vampires were more partial to cities and parties while werewolves preferred the back-to-nature atmosphere of rural living. I just didn't like the crack, that's all. I grew up on a farm, you know. Country breakfasts have a lot to do with my current panoramic physique. Besides, something inside says you shouldn't trust a smiling vampire....or at least you shouldn't trust him too far."

I had been about to mention the fact that I had grown up on a farm, too, but withheld the information. Obviously, farm food hadn't particularly affected my physique, and I didn't want to rob my apprentice of her excuse.

"If he had wanted to do us harm, all he would have had to do was blow the whistle on us while we were still in town," I pointed out. "Let's just take things at face value and assume he was really being as nice as he seemed...for all our peace of minds."

I wished I was as confident as I sounded. We were a long way out in the boondocks, and if Vilhelm had wanted to send us off on a wild goose chase, he couldn't have picked a better direction to start us off in.

"Yeah, well I'd feel a lot better if we weren't being followed," Guido grumbled.

I stopped in my tracks. So did Massha...in her tracks, that is. The bodyguard managed to stumble into us before bringing his own forward progress to a halt.

"What is it, Boss? Something wrong?"

"For a minute there, I thought I heard you say that we were being followed."

"Yeah. Since we left the Dispatcher's. Why does... you mean you didn't know?"

I resisted an impulse to throttle him.

"No, Guido. I didn't know. You see, my bodyguard didn't tell me. He was too busy complaining about the road conditions to have time to mention anything as trivial as someone following us."

Guido took a few shaky steps backward.

"Hey! C'mon, Boss. Don't be like that. I thought you

knew! Honest. Whoever's back there isn't doin' such a hot job of hiding the fact that they're dogging our trail. Any idiot could've spotted...I mean...."

"Keep going, Dark and Deadly," Massha urged. "You're digging yourself in further with every word, in case you hadn't noticed."

With great effort I brought myself back under control.

"Whatever," I said. "I don't suppose you have any idea who it is?"

"Naw. There's only one of 'em. Unless...."

His voice trailed off into silence and he looked suddenly worried.

"Out with it, Guido. Unless what?"

"Well, sometimes when you're getting *really* tricky about tailing someone, you put one real clumsy punk out front so's they can be spotted while you keep your real ace-hitter hidden. I hadn't stopped to think of that before. This turkey behind us could be a decoy, know what I mean?"

"I thought you used decoys for ducks, not turkeys," Massha scowled.

"Well, if that's what's happening, then *we're* sitting ducks, if it makes you feel any better."

"Could both of you just be quiet for a few minutes and let me think?" I said, suddenly impatient with their banter.

"Well, maybe it isn't so bad," Guido said in a doubtful voice. "I'm pretty sure I would have spotted the back-up team if there was one."

"Oh sure," Massha sneered. "Coming out of a town full of vampires that can change themselves into mist whenever they want. Of course you'd spot them."

"Hey. The Boss here can chew on me if he wants, but I don't have to take that from you. You didn't even spot the turkey, remember?"

"The only turkey I can see is...."

"Enough!" I ordered, having arrived at a decision

despite their lack of cooperation. "We have to find out for sure who's behind us and what they want. This is as good a place as any, so I suggest we all retire into the bushes and wait for our shadow to catch up with us....No, Massha. I'll be over here with Guido. You take the other side of the road."

That portion of my plan had less to do with military strategy than with an effort on my part to preserve what little was left of my nerves. I figured the only way to shut the two of them up was to separate them.

"I'm sorry, Boss," Guido whispered as we crouched side by side in the brush. "I keep forgettin' that you aren't as into crime as the boys I usually run with."

Well, I had been half right. Massha on the other side of the road was being quiet, but as long as he had someone to talk to, Guido was going to keep on expressing his thoughts and opinions. I was starting to understand why Don Bruce insisted on doing all the talking when the bodyguards were around. Encouraging employees to speak up as equals definitely had its drawbacks.

"Will you keep your voice down?" I tried once more. "This is supposed to be an ambush."

"Don't worry about that, Boss. It'll be a while before they catch up, and when they do, I'll hear 'em before...."

"Is that you, Skeeve?"

The voice came from the darkness just up the road.

I gave Guido my darkest glare, and he rewarded it with an apologetic shrug that didn't look particularly sincere to me.

Then it dawned on me where I had heard that voice before.

"Right here," I said, rising from my crouch and stepping onto the road. "We've been waiting for you. I think it's about time we had a little chat."

Aside from covering my embarrassment over having been discovered, that had to be my best understatement in quite a while. The last time I had seen this particular person, she was warning me about Aahz's imprisonment.

"Good." She stepped forward to meet me. "That's why I've been following you. I was hoping we could. . . ."

Her words stopped abruptly as Guido and Massha rose from the bushes and moved to join us.

"Well, look who's here," Massha said, flashing one of her less pleasant smiles.

"If it isn't the little bird who sang to the vampires," Guido leered, matching my apprentice's threatening tone.

The girl favored them with a withering glance, then faced me again.

"I was hoping we could talk alone. I've got a lot to say and not much time to say it. It would go faster if we weren't interrupted."

"Not a chance, Sweetheart," Guido snarled. "I'm not goin' to let the Boss out of my sight with you around."

". . . besides which, I've got a few things to tell you myself," Massha added, "like what I think of folks who think frames look better on people than on paintings."

The girl's eyes never left mine. For all her bravado, I thought I could detect in their depths an appeal for help.

"Please," she said softly.

I fought a brief skirmish in my mind, and, as usual, common sense lost.

"All right."

"WHAT! C'mon, Boss. You can't let her get you alone! If her pals are around. . . ."

"Hot Stuff, if I have to sit on you, you aren't going to. . . ."

"Look!" I said, wrenching my eyes away from the girl to confront my mutinous staff. "We'll only go a few steps down the road there, in plain sight. If anything happens you'll be able to pitch in before it gets serious."

"But. . . ."

". . . and you certainly can't think *she's* going to jump me. I mean, it's a cinch she isn't carrying any concealed weapons."

That was a fact. She had changed outfits since the last time I saw her, probably to fit in more with the exotic garb favored by the party-loving vampires. She was wearing what I've heard referred to as a "tank top" which left her midsection and navel delightfully exposed, and the open-sided skirt (if you can call two flaps of cloth that) showed her legs up past her hips. If she had a weapon with her, she had swallowed it. Either that, or . . . .

I dragged my thoughts back to the argument.

"The fact of the matter is that she isn't going to talk in front of a crowd. Now, am I going to get a chance to hear another viewpoint about what's going on, or are we going to keep groping around for information with Aahz's life hanging in the balance?"

My staff fell silent and exchanged glances, each waiting for the other to risk the next blast.

"Well, okay," Massha agreed at last. "But watch yourself, Hot Stuff. Remember, poison can come in pretty bottles."

So, under the ever-watchful glares of my assistants, I retired a few steps down the road for my first words alone with . . . .

"Say, what *is* your name, anyway?"

"Hmmm? Oh. I'm Luanna. Say, thanks for backing me up. That's a pretty mean-looking crew you hang around with. I had heard you had a following, but I hadn't realized how nasty they were."

"Oh, they're okay once you get to know them. If you worked with them on a day-to-day basis, you'd find out that they. . .heck, none of us are really as dangerous or effective as the publicity hype cuts us out to be."

I was suddenly aware of her eyes on me. Her expression was strange. . .sort of a bitter half-smile.

"I've always heard that *really* powerful people tended to understate what they can do, that they don't have to brag. I never really believed it until now."

I really didn't know what to say to that. I mean, my

reputation had gotten big enough that I was starting to get used to being recognized and talked about at the Bazaar, but what she was displaying was neither fear nor envy. Among my own set of friends, admiration or praise was always carefully hidden within our own brand of rough humor or teasing. Faced with the undiluted form of the same thing, I was at a loss as to how to respond.

"Ummm, what was it you wanted to talk to me about?"

Her expression fell and she dropped her eyes.

"This is so embarrassing. Please be patient with me, Skeeve...is it all right if I call you Skeeve? I haven't had much experience with saying 'I'm sorry'...heck, I haven't had much experience with people at all. Just partners and pigeons. Now that I'm here, I really don't know what to say."

"Why don't we start at the beginning?" I wanted to ease her discomfort. "Did you really swindle the Deveels back at the Bazaar?"

Luanna nodded slowly without raising her eyes.

"That's what we do. Matt and me. That and running, even though I think sometimes we're better at running than working scams. Maybe if we were better at conning people, we wouldn't get so much practice at running."

Her words thudded at me like a padded hammer. I had wanted very badly to hear that she was innocent and that it had all been a mistake. I mean, she was so pretty, so sweet, I would have bet my life that she was innocent, yet here she was openly admitting her guilt to me.

"But why?" I managed at last. "I mean, how did you get involved in swindling people to begin with?"

Her soft shoulders rose and fell in a helpless shrug.

"I don't know. It seemed like a good idea when Matt first explained it to me. I was dying to get away from the farm, but I didn't know how to do anything but farmwork for a living...until Matt explained to me how easy it was to get money away from people by playing on their greed.

'Promise them something for nothing,' he said, 'or for so little that they think *they're* swindling *you*.' When he put it that way, it didn't seem so bad. It was more a matter of being smart enough to trick people who thought they were taking advantage of you."

"...by selling them magical items that weren't." I finished for her. "Tell me, why didn't you just go into the magic trade for real?"

Her head came up, and I caught a quick flash of fire in her sad blue eyes.

"We didn't know any magic, so we had to fake it. You probably can't understand that, since you're the real McCoy. I knew that the first time I saw you at Possletum. We were going to try to fake our way into the Court Magician spot until you showed up and flashed a bit of real magic at the crown. Even Matt had to admit that we were outclassed, and we kind of faded back before anyone asked us to show what we could do. I think it was then that I...."

She broke off, giving me a startled, guilty look as if she had been about to say something she shouldn't.

"Go on," I urged, my curiosity piqued.

"It's nothing, really," she said hastily. "Now it's your turn. Since I've told you my story, maybe you won't mind me asking how you got started as a magician."

That set me back a bit. Like her, I had been raised on a farm. I had run away, though, planning to seek my fortune as a master thief, and it was only my chance meeting with my old teacher Garkin and eventually Aahz that had diverted my career goals toward magic. In hindsight, my motives were not discernibly better than hers, but I didn't want to admit it just now. I kind of liked the way she looked at me while laboring under the illusion that I was someone noble and special.

"That's too long a tale to go into just now," I said brusquely. "There are still a few more answers I'd like from you. How come you used our place as a getaway route from Deva?"

"Oh, that was Vic's idea. We teamed up with him just before we started working our con at the Bazaar. When it looked like the scam was starting to turn sour, he said he knew a way-off dimension that no one would be watching. Matt and I didn't even know it was your place until your doorman asked if we were there to see you. Matt was so scared about having to tangle with you that he wanted to forget the whole thing and find another way out, but Vic showed us the door and it looked so easy we just went along with him."

"Of course, it never occurred to you that we'd get stuck with the job of trying to bring you back."

"You better believe it occurred to us. I mean, we didn't think you'd *have* to do it. We expected you'd be mad at us for getting you involved and come after us yourself. Vic kept saying that we shouldn't worry, that if you found us here in Limbo that he could fix it so you wouldn't be able to take us back. I didn't know he was thinking about setting up a frame until he sprang it on your partner."

I tried to let this console me, but it didn't work.

"I notice that once you found out that Aahz was being framed, you still went along with it."

"Well...I didn't want to, but Vic kept saying that if you two were as good as everyone said, that your partner could get out of jail by himself. We figured that he'd escape before the execution, but with the whole dimension hunting him as a fugitive that he'd be too busy running for home to bother about catching us."

I was starting to get *real* anxious to meet this guy Vic. It also occurred to me that of all the potential problems our growing reputation could bring down on us, this was one we had never expected.

"And you believed him?"

Luanna made a face, then shrugged.

"Well...you're supposed to be able to do some pretty incredible things, and I don't want you to think I don't believe in your abilities, but I was worried enough that I sneaked back to let you know what was going on...just in case."

It was almost funny that she was apologizing for giving us the warning. Almost, but not quite. My mind kept running over what might have happened if she *had* believed in me completely.

"I guess my only other question is who is this citizen that Aahz is supposed to have killed?"

"Didn't anybody tell you?" she blinked. "It's Vic. He's from this dimension...you know, a vampire. Anyway, he's hiding out until the whole thing's resolved one way or another. I don't think even Matt knows where he is. Vampires are normally suspicious, and after I sneaked out the first time, he's even gotten cagey around us. He just drops in from time to time to see how we're doing."

Now I *knew* I wanted to meet friend Vic. If I was lucky, I'd meet him before Aahz did.

"Well, I do appreciate you filling me in on the problem. Now, if you'll just come back to Blut with us and explain things to the authorities, my gratitude will be complete."

Luanna started as if I had stuck her with a pin.

"Hold on a minute! Who said anything about going to the authorities? I can't do that! That would be double-crossing *my* partners. I don't want to see you or your friends get hurt, but I can't sacrifice my own to save them."

An honest crook is both incongruous and infuriating. Aahz had often pointed this out to me when some point in my ethic kept me from going along with one of his schemes, and now I was starting to understand what he was talking about.

"But then why are you here?"

"I wanted to warn you. Vic has been thinking that you might come into Limbo after your partner, and he's setting up some kind of trap if you did. If he was right, I thought you should know that you're walking into trouble. I figured that if you came, you'd look up the Dispatcher, so I waited there and followed you when you showed up. I just wanted to warn you is all. That and...."

She dropped her eyes again and lowered her voice until I could hardly hear her.

"...I wanted to see you again. I know it's silly, but...."

As flattering as it was, this time I was unimpressed.

"Yeah, sure." I interrupted. "You're so interested in me you're willing to let my partner sit on a murder rap just so you can watch me go through my paces."

"I already explained about that," she said fiercely, stepping forward to lay a hand on my arm.

I stared at it pointedly until she removed it.

"Well," she said in a small voice. "I can see that there's nothing more I can say. But, Skeeve? Promise me that you won't follow me when I leave? You or your friends? I took a big risk finding you. Please don't make me regret it."

I stared at her for a long moment, then looked away and nodded.

"I know you're disappointed in me, Skeeve," came her voice, "but I can't go against my partners. Haven't you ever had to do something you didn't want to do to support your partner?"

That hit home...painfully.

"Yes, I have," I said, drawing a ragged breath. "I'm sorry, Luanna. I'm just worried about Aahz, that's all. Tell you what. Just to show there're no hard feelings, can I have a token or something? Something to remember you by until I see you again?"

She hesitated, then pulled a gossamer-thin scarf from somewhere inside her outfit. Stepping close, she tucked it into my tunic, then rose on her tiptoes and kissed me softly.

"It's nice of you to ask," she said. "Even if I don't

mean anything to you at all, it's nice of you to ask."

With that, she turned and sprinted off down the road into the darkness.

I stared after her.

"You're letting her go!?"

Suddenly Massha was at my side, flanked by Guido.

"C'mon, Boss. We gotta catch her. She's your partner's ticket off death row. Where's she goin'?"

"To meet up with her partners in crime," I said. "Including a surprisingly lively guy named Vic...surprising since he's the one that Aahz is supposed to have killed."

"So we can catch 'em all together. Nice work, Hot Stuff. Okay, let's follow her and...."

"No!"

"Why not?"

"Because I promised her."

There was a deathly silence as my assistants digested this information.

"So she walks and Green and Scaly dies, is that it?"

"You're sellin' out your partner for a skirt? That musta been some kiss."

I slowly turned to face them, and, mad as they were, they fell silent.

"Now listen close," I said quietly, "because I'm not going to go over it again. If we tried to follow her back to their hideout, and she spotted us, she'd lead us on a wild goose chase and we'd never catch up with them...and we need that so-called corpse. I don't think her testimony alone will swing the verdict."

"But Boss, if we let her get away...."

"We'll find them," I said. "Without us dogging her footsteps, she'll head right back to her partners."

"But how will we...."

In answer, I pulled Luanna's scarf from my tunic.

"Fortunately, she was kind enough to provide us with a means to track her, once we recruit the necessary werewolf."

Guido gave my back a slap that almost staggered me.

"Way to go, Boss," he crowed. "You really had me goin' for a minute. I thought that chickie had really snowed you."

I looked up to find Massha eyeing me suspiciously.

"That *was* quite a kiss, Hot Stuff," she said. "If I didn't know better, I'd think that young lady is more than a little stuck on you . . . and you just took advantage of it."

I averted my eyes, and found myself staring down the road again.

"As a wise woman once told me," I said, "sometimes you have to do things you don't like to support your partner . . . . Now, let's go find these Woof Writers."

# Chapter IX

*"My colleagues and I feel that
independents like ElfQuest
are nothing but sheep in
wolves' clothing!"*

S. Lee

THE Woof Writers turned out to be much more pleasant than I had dared hope, which was fortunate as my were-wolf disguises were some of the shakiest I'd ever done. Guido was indeed allergic to werewolves as feared (he started sneezing a hundred yards from their house) and was waiting outside, but even trying to maintain two disguises was proving to be a strain on my powers in this magic-poor dimension. I attempted to lessen the drain by keeping the changes minimal, but only succeeded in making them incredibly unconvincing even though my assistants assured me they were fine. No matter what anyone tells you, believe, me, pointy ears alone do not a wolf make.

You might wonder why I bothered with disguises at all? Well, frankly, we were getting a little nervous. Everyone we had talked to or been referred to in this dimension was so *nice*! We kept waiting for the other shoe to drop. All of our talks and discussions of possible traps had made us so skittish that we were now convinced that there was going to be a double-cross somewhere along the way. The only question in our minds was when and by whom.

With that in mind, we decided it would be best to try to pass ourselves off as werewolves until we knew for sure the Woof Writers were as well-disposed toward humans as Vilhelm said they were. The theory was that if they weren't, the disguises might give us a chance to get out again before our true nature was exposed. The only difficulty with that plan was that I had never seen a werewolf in my life, so not only was I working with a shortage of energy, I was unsure as to what the final result should look like. As it turned out, despite their knowledgeable advice, my staff didn't know either.

While we're answering questions from the audience, you might ask, if neither I nor my assistants knew what a werewolf looked like, how I knew the disguises were inadequate? Simple. I deduced the fact after one look at real werewolves. That and the Woof Writers told me so. Didn't I tell you they were great folks? Of course, they let us sweat for a while before admitting that they knew we were poorly disguised humans all along, but I myself tend to credit that to their dubious sense of humor. It's Massha who insists it was blatant sadism. Of course, she was the one who had to eat a bone before they acknowledged the joke.

Anyway, I was talking about the Woof Writers. It was interesting in that I had never had much opportunity to watch a husband-wife team in action before (my parents don't count). The closest thing to the phenomenon I had witnessed was the brother-sister team of Tananda and Chumley, but they spent most of their conversational time tyring to "one-down" each other. The Woof Writers, in contrast, seemed to take turns playing "crazy partner-sane partner." They never asked my opinion, but I felt that she was much better at playing the crazy than he. He was so good at playing the straight that when he did slip

into crazy mode, it always came as a surprise.

"Really, dear," Idnew was saying to Massha, "wouldn't you like to slip out of that ridiculous disguise into something more comfortable? A werewolf with only two breasts looks so silly."

"Idnew," her husband said sternly, "you're making our guests uncomfortable. Not everyone feels as easy about discussing their bodies as you do."

"It's the artist in me," she returned. "And besides, Drahcir, who was it that set her up to eat a bone?—and an old one at that. If you were a little more conscientious when you did the shopping instead of stocking up on junk food...."

"Oh, don't worry about me, Hairy and Handsome," Massha interceded smoothly, dropping into her vamp role. "I've got no problems discussing my body, as long as we get equal time to talk about yours. I've always liked my men with a lot of facial hair, if you get my drift."

I noticed Idnew's ears flatten for a moment before returning to their normal upright position. While it may have been nothing more than a nervous twitch, it occurred to me that if we were going to solicit help from these two, it might not be wise to fan any embers of jealousy that might be lying about.

"Tell me," I said hastily, eager to get the subject away from Massha's obvious admiration of Drahcir, "What got you started campaigning for better relationships between humans and werewolves?"

"Well, there were many factors involved," Drahcir explained, dropping into the lecturer mode I had grown to know so well in such a short time. "I think the most important thing to keep in mind is that the bad reputation humans have is vastly overrated. There is actually very little documented evidence to support the legends of human misconduct. For the most part, werewolves tend to forget that, under the proper conditions, we turn into humans. Most of them are afraid or embarrassed and hide themselves away until it passes, but Idnew and I don't. If anything we generally seize the opportunity to go out and about and get the public used to seeing harmless humans in their midst. Just between us, though, I think Idnew here likes to do it because it scares the hell out of folks to be suddenly confronted by a human when they aren't expecting it. In case you haven't noticed, there's a strong exhibitionist streak in my wife. For myself, it's simply a worthy cause that's been neglected for far too long."

"The other factor, which my husband has neglected to mention," Idnew put in impishly, "is that there's a lot of money in it."

"There is?" I asked.

My work with Aahz had trained me to spot profit opportunities where others saw none, but this time the specific angle had eluded me.

"There...umm...are certain revenues to be gleaned from our campaign," Drahcir said uneasily, shooting a dark glance at his wife. "T-shirts, bumper stickers, lead miniatures, fan club dues, greeting cards, and calendars, just to name a few. It's a dirty job, but somebody's got to do it. Lest my wife leave you with the wrong impression of me, however, let me point out that I'm supporting this particular cause because I *really* believe in it. There are lots of ways to make money."

"...and he knows them all, don't you dear?" Idnew said with a smile.

"Really?" I interrupted eagerly. "Would you mind running over a few? Could I take notes?"

"Before you get carried away, High Roller," Massha warned, "remember why we came here originally."

"Oh! Right! Thanks, Massha. For a minute there I...Right!"

It took me a few seconds to rechannel my thoughts. While Aahz's training has gotten me out of a lot of tight spots and generally improved my standard of living, there are some unfortunate side effects.

Once I got my mind back on the right track, I quickly filled the werewolves in on our current problem. I kept the details sketchy, both because I was getting tired of going back and forth over the same beginning, and to keep from having to elaborate on Luanna's part in causing our dilemma. Still, the Woof Writers seemed quite enthralled by the tale, and listened attentively until I was done.

"Gee, you're really in a spot," Idnew said when I finally ground to a halt. "If there's anything we can do to help...."

"We can't," Drahcir told us firmly. "You're behind on your deadlines, Idnew, and I've got three more appearances this month...not to mention answering the mail that's piled up the last two weekends I've been gone."

"Drahcir...." Idnew said, drawing out his name.

"Don't look at me like that, dear," her husband argued before she had even started her case, "and don't cock your head, either. Someone's liable to shove a gramophone under it. Remember, *you're* the one who keeps pointing out that we have to put more time into our work."

"I was talking about cutting back on your personal appearances," Idnew argued. "Besides, this is important."

"So's meeting our deadlines. I'm as sympathetic to their problem as you are, but we can't let the plight of one small group of humans interfere with our work on the big picture."

"But *you're* the one who insists that deadlines aren't as important as...."

She broke off suddenly and semaphored her ears toward her husband.

"Wait a minute. Any time you start talking about 'big pictures' and 'grand crusades'...is our bank account low again?"

Drachir averted his eyes and shifted his feet uncomfortably.

"Well, I was going to tell you, but I was afraid it might

80

distract you while you were trying to work...."

"All right. Let's have it," his wife growled, her hackles rising slightly. "What is it you've invested our money in this time?"

I was suddenly very uncomfortable. Our little discussion seemed to be dissolving into a family fight I felt I had no business being present for. Apparently Massha felt the same thing.

"Well, if you can't help us, that's that," she said, getting to her feet. "No problem. A favor's not a favor if you have to be argued into it. C'mon, Hot Stuff. We're wasting our time *and* theirs."

Though in part I agreed with her, desperation prompted me to make one last try.

"Not so fast, Massha. Drachir is right. Time's money. Maybe we could work out some kind of a fee to compensate them for their time in helping us. Then it's not a favor, it's a business deal. Face it, we *really* need their help in this. The odds of us finding this Vic character on our own are pretty slim."

Aahz would have fainted dead away if he had heard me admitting how much we needed help *before* the fee was set, but that reaction was nothing compared to how the Woof Writers took my offer.

"What did you say?" Drahcir demanded, rising to all fours with his ears back.

"I said that maybe you'd help us if we offered to pay you," I repeated, backing away slightly. "I didn't mean to insult you...."

"You can't insult Drahcir with money," his wife snapped. "He meant what did you say about Vic?"

"Didn't I mention him before?" I frowned. "He's the vampire that Aahz is supposed to have...."

There was a sudden loud flapping sound in the rafters above our heads, like someone noisily shaking a newspaper to scare a cat off a table. It worked...not on the cat (I don't think the werewolves owned one) but on Massha

81

and me. My apprentice hit the floor, covering her head with her hands, while I, more used to sudden danger and being more svelte and agile, dove beneath the coffee table.

By the time we recovered from our panicky...excuse me, our shrewd defensive maneuvers, there was nothing to see except the vague shape of someone with huge wings disappearing out the front door.

"This one's all yours, dear," Drahcir said firmly, his posture erect and unmoved despite the sudden activity.

"Come on, honey," his wife pleaded. "You're so much better at explaining things. You're supposed to help me out when it comes to talking to people."

"It's a skill I polished at those personal appearances you're so critical of," he retorted stiffly.

"Would *somebody* tell me what's going on?" I said in tones much louder than I usually use when I'm a guest in someone's home.

Before I could get an answer, the door burst open again utterly destroying what little was left of my nervous system.

"Hey, Boss! Did you s—se—Wha—wa...."

"Outside, Guido!" I ordered, glad to have someone I could shout at without feeling guilty. "Blow your nose... and I'm *fine,* thanks! Nice of you to ask!"

By the time my bodyguard had staggered back outside, his face half buried in a handkerchief, I had managed to regain most of my composure.

"Sorry for the interruption," I said as nonchalantly as I could, "but my colleague *does* raise an interesting question. What *was* that?"

"Scary?" Massha suggested.

Apparently she had recovered her composure a little better than I had. I closed my eyes and reflected again on the relative value of cheeky apprentices.

"*That,*" Drahcir said loftily, barely in time to keep me from my assistant's throat, "was Vic...one of my wife's weird artist friends who dropped in unannounced for a prolonged stay *and,* unless I miss my guess, the criminal you're looking for who framed your partner."

"He wasn't really a friend of mine," Idnew put in in a small voice. "Just a friend of a friend, really. Weird artist types tend to stick together and pass around the locations of crash spaces. He was just another charity case down on his luck who...."

"...who is currently winging his way back to his accomplice with the news that we're on their trail," I finished with a grimace.

"Isn't that 'accomplices" as in plural?" Massha asked softly.

I ignored her.

"Oh, Drahcir," Idnew said, "now we have to help them. It's the only way we can make up for having provided a hideout for the very person they were trying to find."

"If I might point out," her husband replied, "we've barely met these people. We don't really owe them an explanation, much less any help. Besides, you still have a deadline to meet and...."

"Drahcir!" Idnew interrupted. "It could get real lonely sleeping in the old kennel while I work day and night on a deadline, if you catch my meaning."

"Now, dear," Drahcir said, sidling up to his wife, "before you go getting into a snit, hear me out. I've been thinking it over and I think there's a way we can provide assistance without biting into our own schedules. I mean, we *do* have a friend...one who lives a little north of here...who's temporarily between assignments and could use the work. I'm sure he'd be willing to do a little tracking for them at a fraction of the fee that we'd charge for the same service."

He was obviously talking in the veiled references partners use to communicate or check ideas in front of strangers, as his words went completely over my head, but drew an immediate reaction from Idnew.

"Oh, Drahcir!" she exclaimed excitedly, all trace of her earlier anger gone. "That's perfect! And he'll just *love* Massha."

"There's still the question of whether or not we can get him here in time," her husband cautioned. "And of course I'll want a percentage off the top as a finder's fee...."

"WHAT!" I exclaimed.

"I agree," Idnew said firmly. "A finder's fee is totally...."

"No! Before that," I urged. "What did you say about there not being enough time? I thought the execution wasn't scheduled until the end of the week!"

"That's right," Drahcir said. "But the end of the week is tomorrow. Your friend is slated to be executed at high midnight."

"C'mon, Massha," I ordered, heading for the door. "We're heading back to Blut."

"What for?" she demanded. "What can we do without a tracker?"

"We've tried being nice about this, and it isn't working," I responded grimly. "Now we do it the other way. You wanted action, apprentice? How do you feel about giving me a hand with a little jailbreak?"

# Chapter X

*"What's wrong with a little*
*harmless crime once in a while?"*
**M. Blaise**

$B$UT I'm telling you, Boss, jailbreak is a bad rap. With you operating at only half power in the magic department, there's no tellin' what can go wrong, and then...."

"Before we get all worked up about what can go wrong, Guido," I said, trying to salvage something constructive out of the conversation, "could you give me a little information on exactly how hard it is to break someone out of jail? Or haven't you been involved in any jailbreaks, either?"

"Of course I've been along on some jailbreaks," the bodyguard declared, drawing himself up proudly. "I've been an accomplice on *three* jailbreaks. What kind of Mob member do you take me for, anyway?"

With a heroic effort I resisted the temptation to answer that particular rhetorical question.

"Okay. So how about a few pointers? This is my first jailbreak, and I want it to go right."

I was all set to settle in for a fairly lengthy lecture, but instead of launching into the subject, Guido looked a bit uncomfortable.

"Umm...actually, Boss, I don't think you'd want to use any of the plans I followed. You see, all three of 'em were busts. None of 'em worked, and in two of the capers, the guy we were tryin' to save got killed. That's how I know about what a bad rap a jailbreak is, know what I mean?"

"Oh, swell! Just swell! Tell me, *Mister* bodyguard, with your allergies and zero-for-three record at jailbreak, did you ever do *anything* for the Mob that worked?"

A gentle hand fell on my shoulder from behind.

"Hey! Ease up a little, High Roller," Massha said softly. "I know you're worried about your partner, but don't take it out on Guido...or me, either, for that matter. We may not be much, but we're here and trying to help as best we can when we'd both just as soon be back at the Bazaar. You're in a bad enough spot without starting a two-front war by turning on your allies."

I started to snap at her, but caught myself in time. Instead, I drew a long ragged breath and blew it out slowly. She was right. My nerves were stretched to the breaking point...which served me right for not following my own advice.

We were currently holed up at the Dispatcher's, the only place I could think of for an in-town base of operations, and as soon as we had arrived, I had insisted that both Massha and Guido grab a bit of sleep. We had been going nonstop ever since stepping through the door into Limbo, and I figured that the troops would need all the rest they could get before we tried to spring Aahz. Of course, once I had convinced them of the necessity of racking out, I promptly ignored my own wisdom and stayed up thinking for the duration.

The rationalization I used for this insane action was that I wanted some extra time uninterrupted to recharge my internal batteries, so whatever minimal magic I had at my disposal would be ready for our efforts. In actuality, what I did was worry. While I had indeed taken part in several criminal activities since teaming up with Aahz, they had all been planned by either Aahz or Tananda. This was my first time to get involved in masterminding a caper, and the stakes were high. Not only Aahz's but Massha's and Guido's futures were riding on my successful debut, and my confidence level was at an all-time low. After much pondering, I had decided to swallow my pride and lean heavily on Guido's expertise, which was why it hit me so hard when I discovered that he knew even less about successful jailbreaks than I.

"Sorry, Guido," I said, trying to restructure my thinking. "I guess I'm more tired than I realized. Didn't mean to snap at you."

"Don't worry, Boss," the bodyguard grinned. "I've been expectin' it. All the big operators I've worked with get a little crabby when the heat's on. If anything, your temper gettin' short is the best thing I've seen since we started this caper. That's why I've been so jumpy myself. I wasn't sure if you weren't taking the job seriously, or if you were just too dumb to know the kind of odds we were up against. Now that you're acting normal for the situation, I feel a lot better about how it's goin' to come out in the end."

Terrific! Now that I was at the end of my rope, our eternal pessimist thought things were going great.

"Okay," I said, rubbing my forehead with one finger, "we haven't got much information to go on, and what we do know is bad. According to Vilhelm, Aahz is being held in the most escape-proof cell they have, which is the top floor of the highest tower in town. If we try to take him from the inside, we're going to have to fool or fight every guard on the way up *and* down. To me, that means our best bet is to spring him from the outside."

My assistants nodded vigorously, their faces as enthusiastic as if I had just said something startlingly original and clever.

"Now, with my powers at low ebb, I don't think I can

levitate that far *and* spring the cell. Massha, do you have anything in your jewelry collection that would work for rope and climbing hooks?"

"N—no," she said hesitantly, which surprised me. She usually had a complete inventory of her nasty pretties on the tip of her tongue.

"I saw a coil of rope hangin' just inside the door," Guido supplied.

"I noticed it, too," I acknowledged, "but it isn't nearly long enough. We'll just have to use up my power getting up to the cell and figure some other way of opening the window."

"Ummm...you don't have to do that, High Roller," Massha said with a sigh. "I've got something we can use."

"What's that?"

"The belt I'm wearing with all my gear hung on it. It's a levitation belt. The controls aren't horribly reliable, but it should do to get us to the top of the tower."

I cocked an eyebrow at my apprentice.

"Wait a minute, Massha. Why didn't you mention this when I asked?"

She looked away quickly.

"You didn't ask about a belt. Only about rope and climbing hooks."

"Since when do I have to ask you specific questions ...or any questions, for that matter, to get your input?"

"All right," she sighed. "If you really want to know, I was hoping we could find a way to do this without using the belt."

"Why?"

"It embarrasses me."

"It what?"

"It embarrasses me. I look silly floating around in the air. It's okay for skinny guys like you and Guido, but when I try it, I look like a blimp. All I'd need is Goodyear tattooed on my side to make the picture complete."

I closed by eyes and tried to remember that I was tired

and that I shouldn't take it out on my friends. The fact that Massha was worried about appearances while I was trying to figure out a way to get us all out of this alive wasn't really infuriating. It was...flattering! That was it! She was so confident of my abilities to get us through this crisis that she had time to think about appearances! Of course, the possibility of betraying that confidence set me off in another round of worrying. Wonderful.

"You okay, Boss?"

"Hmmm? Yeah. Sure, Guido. Okay. Now Massha floats up to the window, which leaves you and me free to...."

"Hold it, Hot Stuff," Massha said, holding up a hand. "I think I'd better explain a little more about this belt. I bought it in an 'as-is' rummage sale, and the controls are not all they should be."

"How so?"

"Well, the 'up' control works okay, but the 'altitude' is shaky so you're never sure how much you can lift or how high it will go. The real problem, though, is the 'down' control. There's no tapering-off effect, so it's either on or off."

I was never particularly good at technical jargon, but flying was something I knew so I could almost follow her.

"Let me see if I've got this right," I said. "When you go up, you aren't sure how much power you'll have, and when you land...."

"...it ain't gentle," she finished for me. "Basically, you fall from whatever height you're at to the ground."

"I don't know much about this magic stuff," Guido commented dryly, "but that doesn't sound so good. Why would you use a rig like that, anyway?"

"I don't...at least not for flying," Massha said. "Remember, I told you I think it makes me look silly? All I use it for is a utility belt...you know, like Batman? I mean, it's kind of pretty, and it isn't easy to find belts in my size."

"Whatever," I said, breaking into their fashion discussion. "We're going to use it tonight to get up to the cell even if it means rigging some kind of ballast system. Now all we need to figure out is how to open the cell window and a getaway plan. Guido, it occurs to me that we might pick up a few lessons on jailbreaks from your experiences even if they *were* unsuccessful. I mean, negative examples can be as instructive as positive examples. So tell me, in your opinion what went wrong in the plans you followed in the past?"

The bodyguard's brow furrowed as it took on the unaccustomed exercise of thought.

"I dunno, Boss. It seems that however much planning was done, something always came up that we hadn't figured on. If I had to hang our failures on any one thing, I'd say it was just that...overplanning. I mean, after weeks of lectures and practice sessions, you get a little overconfident, so when something goes wrong you're caught flatfooted, know what I mean?"

Nervous as we were, that got a laugh from both Massha and me.

"Well, that's one problem we won't have to worry about," I said. "Our planning time is *always* minimal, and for this caper we're going to have to put it together in a matter of hours."

"If you take hours, you'll never pull it off," Vilhelm said, entering our planning room just in time to hear my last comment.

"What's that supposed to mean?" Massha growled.

"Say, are you *sure* you guys are on the level?" the vampire said, ignoring my apprentice. "It occurs to me that I've only got your word on all this...that Vic is still alive and all. If you're taking advantage of my good nature to get me involved in something crooked...."

"He's alive," I assured him. "I've seen him myself since we were here last...but you didn't answer the question. What was that you were saying about what

90

would happen if we took hours to plan the jailbreak?"

The Dispatcher shrugged.

"I suppose you guys know what you're doing and I should keep my mouth shut, but I was getting a little worried. I mean, it's sundown already, and if you're going to make your move before the execution, it had better be soon."

"How do you figure that?" I frowned. "The action isn't slated until high midnight. I had figured on waiting a while until it was dark and things quieted down around town a little."

"Are you kidding?" the vampire said with a start, his eyebrows going up to his hairline. "That's when...oh, I get it. You're still thinking in terms of your off-dimension timetables. You've got to...umm, you might want to be sitting down for this, Skeeve."

"Lay it on me," I said, rubbing my forehead again. "What have I overlooked now? Even without the blindfold and the cigarette I'd just as soon take the bad news standing up."

"Well, you've got to remember that you're dealing with a city of vampires here. Sundown is the equivalent of dawn to us. That's when things *start* happening, not when they start winding down! That means...."

"...that high midnight is a major traffic time and the longer we wait, the more people there will be on the street," I said, trying to suppress a groan.

Once the basic oversight had been pointed out, I could do my own extrapolations...with all their horrible consequences. Trying to fight back my own panic, I turned to my assistants.

"Okay, troops. We're on. Guido, grab that rope you saw. We may need it before this is over."

The bodyguard's eyes widened with astonishment.

"You mean we're going to start the caper right now? But Boss! We haven't planned...."

"Hey, Guido," I said, flashing a grin that was almost

sane. "you were the one who said that overplanning was a problem. Well, if you're right, this should be the most successful jailbreak ever!"

# Chapter XI

*"Nice jail. Looks strong."*
**H. Houdini**

VILHELM was right about one thing. The streets were nowhere nearly as crowded as they had been the times we navigated their length well after sundown. Only a few stray beings wandered here and there, mostly making deliveries or sweeping down the sidewalks in front of their shops prior to opening. Except for the lack of light, the streets looked just like any town preparing for a day's business...that and the red eyes of the citizens.

We hugged the light as we picked our way across town....

That's right. I said "hugged the light." I try to only make the same mistake a dozen times. In other dimensions, we would have "hugged the dark" to avoid being noticed or recognized. Here, we "hugged the light." Don't laugh. It worked.

Anyway, as we picked our way through the streets of Blut, most of my attention was taken up with the task of trying to map a good getaway route. Getting Aahz out of jail I would deal with once we got there. Right now I was worried about what we would do once we had him out...a major assumption, I know, but I had so little optimism that I clung to what there was with all fours.

The three of us looked enough like vampires in appearance to pass casual inspection. There was no way, however, that we could pass off my scaly green partner as a native without a disguise spell, and I wasn't about to bet on having any magical energy left after springing Aahz. As such, I was constantly craning my neck to peer down side-streets and alleys, hoping to find a little-traveled route by which we could spirit our fugitive colleague out of town without bringing the entire populace down on our necks. By the time we reached our destination, I was pretty sure I could get us back to the Dispatcher's by the route we were following, and *positively* sure that if I tried to take us there by the back routes, I would get us totally and help-lessly lost.

"Well, Boss. This is it. Think we can crack it?"

I don't think Guido really expected an answer. He was just talking to break the silence that had fallen over us as we stood looking at our target.

The Municipal Building was an imposing structure, with thick stone walls and a corner tower that stretched up almost out of sight into the darkness. It didn't look like we could put a dent in it with a cannon...if we had a cannon, which we didn't. I was used to the tents of the Bazaar or the rather ramshackle building style of Klah. While I had been gradually getting over being overawed by the construction prevalent here in Blut, this place intimidated me. I'd seen shakier looking mountains!

"Well, one thing's for certain," I began, almost under my breath.

"What's that?"

"Staring at it isn't going to make it any weaker."

Neither of my assistants laughed at my joke, but then again, neither did I.

Shaking off a feeling of foreboding, I turned to my staff.

"All right, Guido. You stay down here and keep

94

watch. Massha? Do you think that belt of yours can lift two? It's time I went topside and took a good look at this impregnable cell."

My apprentice licked her lips nervously and shrugged.

"I don't know, Hot Stuff. I warned you that the controls on this thing don't work right. It could lift us right into orbit for all I know."

I patted her shoulder in what I hoped was a reassuring way.

"Well, give it a try and we'll find out."

She nodded, wrapped one arm around my chest, and used her other hand to play with the jewels on her belt buckle.

There was a sparkle of light, but beyond that nothing.

"Not enough juice," she mumbled to herself.

"So turn it up already," I urged.

Even if the vampires tended to avoid light, we were lit up like a Christmas tree and bound to attract attention if we stayed at ground level much longer.

"Cross your fingers," she said grimly and touched the jewels again.

The light intensified and we started up fast...too fast.

"Careful, Boss!" Guido shouted and grabbed my legs as they went past him.

That brought our progress to a halt...well, almost. Instead of rocketing up into the night, we were rising slowly, almost imperceptibly.

"That's got it, High Roller!" Massha exclaimed, shifting her grip to hang onto me with both arms. "A little more ballast than I had planned on, though."

I considered briefly telling Guido to let go, but rejected the thought. If the bodyguard released his grip, we'd doubtless resume our previous speed...and while a lot of folks at the Bazaar talked about my meteoric rise, I'd just as soon keep the phrase figurative. There was also the minor detail that we were already at a height where it would be dangerous for Guido to try dropping back to the street. There was that, and his death-grip on my legs.

"Don't tell me, let me guess," I called down to him. "You're acrophobic, too?"

The view of Blut that was unfolding beneath us was truly breathtaking. Truly! My life these days was so cluttered with crisis and dangers that a little thing like looking down on buildings didn't bother me much, but even I was finding it hard to breathe when confronted up close with sheer walls adorned with stone creatures. Still, until I felt his fingernails biting into my calves, it had never occurred to me that such things might upset a rough-and-tumble guy like Guido.

"Naw. I got nothin' against spiders," he replied nervously. "It's heights that scare me."

I let that one go. I was busy studying the tower which could be viewed much more clearly from this altitude. If anything, it looked stronger than the portion of the building that was below us. One feature captured my attention, though. The top portion of the tower, the part I assumed was Aahz's cell, was shaped like a large dragon's head. The window I had been expecting was actually the creature's mouth, with its teeth serving as bars.

I should have anticipated something like that, realizing the abundance of stone animals on every other building in town. Still, it came as a bit of a surprise...but a pleasant surprise. I had been trying to figure a way to get through iron bars, but stone teeth might be a bit easier. Maybe with Aahz working from the inside and us working from the outside, we could loosen the mortar and. . . .

I suddenly realized that in a few moments we would be level with the cell...and that a few moments after that we'd be past it! Unless something was done, and done fast, to halt our upward progress, we'd only have time for a few quick words with Aahz before parting company permanently. With time running out fast, I cast about for a solution.

The wall was too far away to grab onto, and there was no way to increase our weight, unless. . . .

When Aahz first taught me to fly, he explained the process as "levitation in reverse." That is, instead of using the mind to lift objects, you push against the ground and lift yourself. Focusing my reservoir of magical energy, I used a small portion to try *flying* in reverse. Instead of pushing up, I pushed down!

Okay. So I was desperate. In a crisis, I'll try anything, however stupid. Fortunately, this stupid idea worked!

Our upward progress slowed to a halt with me hanging at eye-level with the cell's dragon mouth.

Trying not to show my relief, I raised my voice.

"Hey, Aahz! When are visiting hours?"

For a moment there was no response, and I had a sudden fear that we were hanging a hundred feet in the air outside an empty cell. Then my partner's unmistakable countenance appeared in the window.

"Skeeve?" he said in a skeptical voice. "Skeeve! What are you doing out there?"

"Oh, we were just in the neighborhood and thought we'd drop in," I replied in my best nonchalant voice. "Heard you were in a bit of trouble and thought we'd better get you out before it got serious."

"Who's we?" my partner demanded, then he focused on my assistants. "Oh no! Those two? Where are Tananda and Chumley? C'mon, Skeeve. I need a rescue team and you bring me a circus act!"

"It's the best I could do on short notice," I shot back, slightly annoyed. "Tananda and Chumley aren't back from their own work yet, but I left a message for them to catch up with us if they could. Of course, I'm not sure how much help they'll be. In case you're wondering why I'm being carried by my apprentice instead of flying free, this particular dimension is exceptionally low on force lines to tap in to. If anything, I think I'm pretty lucky that I brought 'these two' along instead of ending up with a

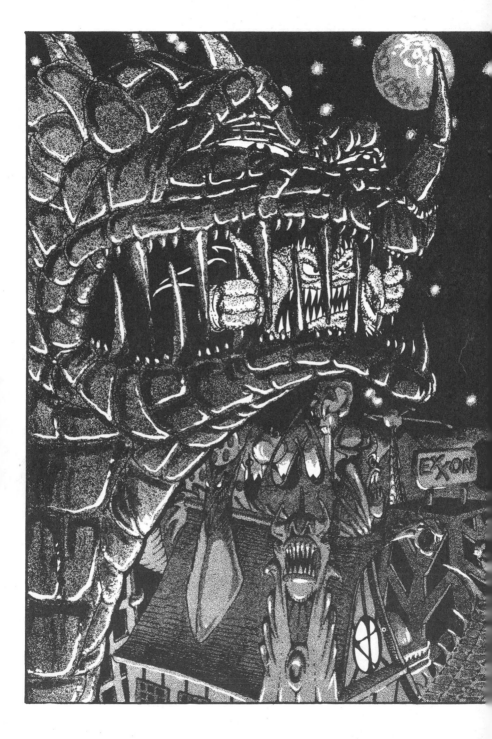

whole team of for-real magicians who are too proud to use gimmicks. It's thanks to 'these two' that I made it this far at all. Now, do you want our help, or do you want to wait for the next team to float past? I mean, you're in no rush, are you?"

"Now don't get your back up, partner," Aahz said soothingly. "You caught me a little off-guard is all. So tell me, just how do you figure to get me out of here?"

That brought me back to earth...or as close to it as I could get while suspended in mid-air.

"Umm...actually, Aahz, I was kinda hoping *you* might have a few ideas on the subject. You're usually pretty good at coming up with plans to get us out of tight spots."

"What I want to know," Guido snarled, turning slightly in the wind, "is how come your partner hasn't figured a way out of there all by himself, if he's so all-fired smart?"

I started to rebuke my bodyguard, but slowly his words sank in. That was a good question! Aahz was strong...I mean STRONG! By rights he should have been able to rip the stone teeth out of the window all by himself. What *was* keeping him here?

"Oh, I'm having so much fun in here I just couldn't bear to leave," Aahz barked back. "I'm in here because I can't get out, that's why. What's more, if any of you have any ideas about how to get me out, I think now's a real good time to share them with the rest of us."

"Wait a minute, Aahz," I said. "*Why* can't you get out...and how did they catch you in the first place?"

"I was framed," my partner retorted, but I noticed his voice was a bit more subdued.

"We already know that," I pressed. "What I want to know is why you didn't just bust a few heads and sprint for home? You've never been particularly respectful of local authority before."

To my surprise, Aahz actually looked embarrassed.

"I was drugged," he said in a disgusted tone. "They put something in my drink, and the next thing I knew I had a stake and mallet in my hands and a room full of officials. Whatever it was they used, it kept me groggy all the way through the trial...I mean I couldn't walk straight, much less defend myself coherently, and after that I was in *here*!"

"The old Mickey Finn trick!" Massha snorted, rocking our entire formation. "I'm surprised someone as off-worldly as you could get caught by such a corny stunt."

"Yeah. It surprised me, too!" Aahz admitted. "I mean, that gag is so old, who would really expect anyone to try it at all?"

"Only if you figured the mark was louder than he was smart," Guido sneered.

"Is that so!" my partner snapped, ready to renew their old rivalry. "Well, when I get out of here, you and me can...."

"Stop it, you two," I ordered. "Right now the problem is to get us *all* out of here before the balloon goes up...no offense, Massha. Now spill, Aahz. What's so special about this cell that's keeping you bottled up?"

My partner heaved a great sigh.

"Take another look at it, Skeeve. A *close* look."

I did. It still looked the same to me: a tower room on the shape of a dragon's head.

"Yeah. Okay. So?"

"So remember where we are. This thing was built to hold *vampire* criminals. You know, beings with super-human strength that can change into mist?"

My gaze flew back to the dragon's head.

"I don't get it," I admitted. "How can any stone cell hold beings like that?"

"That's the point." Aahz winced. "A stone cell *can't*! This thing is made of *living* stone. If whoever's inside tries to bust out, it swallows them. If they try to turn into mist, it inhales them."

"You mean...."

"Now you're getting the picture."

He flashed his toothy grin at me despite his obvious depression.

"The cell is alive!"

Startled by this revelation, I looked at the tower top cell again. As if it had been waiting for the right cue, the dragon's head opened its eyes and looked at me.

# Chapter XII

*"For the right person,*
*the impossible is easy!"*

**Dumbo**

To everyone's surprise, particularly my own, I didn't find the revelation about the true nature of Aahz's confinement at all discouraging. If anything, I was doubly pleased. Not only did I have an immediate idea for how to beat the problem, I had arrived at it before my knowledgeable partner... well before, as a matter of fact, as he had been pondering his dilemma for days whereas I had only just received the information. Of course, he was probably not in a position to see the easy solution that I could.

"What are you grinning at?" he demanded. "If there's anything funny about this, it eludes me completely."

Unlike my own amiable self, Aahz tends to show his worry by getting mad. Come to think of it, he tends to express almost any emotion by *getting* mad. Well, at least he's consistent.

"Tell me," I said, eyeing the dragon's head, "you say this thing's alive. How alive is it?"

"What do you mean, 'how alive is it'?" Aahz scowled. "It's alive enough to swallow me if it gets it into it's head. That's alive enough for me.

"I mean, can it hear and see?"

"Who cares?" my partner said, in a dazzling display of charm and curiosity that makes him so lovable. "I hadn't planned on asking it out for a date."

I stared thoughtfully at the beast.

"I was just wondering if it could hear me. . .say, if I said that I thought it was the ugliest building decoration I've seen here in town?"

The dragon's head rewarded me by narrowing its eyes into an evil glare.

"I think it can hear you, Boss," Guido said, shifting his grip nervously. "It doesn't look like it liked that last comment."

"Oh, swell!" Aahz grumbled. "Tell you what, partner. Why don't *you* come in here and sit on this thing's tongue instead of me before you start getting it all riled up?"

"I was just checking." I smiled. "To tell the truth, I think it's the most incredible thing I've seen since I started traveling the dimensions. I just said that other to test its reactions."

The dragon stopped glaring, but it still looked a little bit suspicous and wary.

"Well, find some other reaction to test, okay?" my partner snapped. "For some obscure reason, I'm a little nervous these days, and every time this thing moves its tongue I age a few centuries."

I ignored his grumbling and shook one of my legs.

"Hey, Guido! Are you still paying attention down there?"

His grip tightened fiercely.

"Of course I'm paying attention, you little. . .I mean, yeah, Boss. There's not much else to do while we're hangin' here, know what I mean? And quit jerking your leg around. . .please?"

I found his verbal slip rather interesting, but now wasn't the time to investigate further.

"Well, listen up," I said. "Here's what I want you to

do. I want you to let go with one hand and pass the rope up to me...."

"No way, Boss! Have you seen how far down it is? I'm not lettin' go no matter what you...."

"...because if you don't," I continued as if he hadn't interrupted, "I'm going to start squirming around until either you lose your grip with both hands or Massha loses her grip on me. Whichever way it goes, you'll fall. Get my drift? Now for once could you just follow orders without a lot of back-talk? We don't have much time to pull this off."

There was a stricken silence below as Guido absorbed my ultimatum and weighed the possibilities.

"Pull what off?" Aahz demanded. "Why doesn't anybody tell me anything? If this master plan of yours is riding on that sorry excuse for a bodyguard, you might as well give up right now. I've told you all along that he was too lily-livered to be any good at...."

"Who's lily-livered?!" Guido shouted. "Look, Big Mouth, as soon as we get you out of there, you and me are going to settle this once and...."

"First, we've got to get him out, Guido," I interrupted. "The rope."

"Right, Boss. One rope coming up. We'll see who's lily-livered. The last person who called me that was my mom, and by the time I got done with her...."

Our whole formation began to rock dangerously as he fumbled through his coat one-handed in search of the rope. For a minute, I was afraid he was mad enough to let go with both hands to speed his search.

"Easy there, Guido," I cautioned. "We can...."

"Here it is, Boss!" he said, flipping the rope up so violently that it almost whacked me in the face. "I hope you can use it to hang the son of a...."

"Hanging isn't enough!" Aahz taunted. "It takes more than a piece of rope to do me in."

"Yeah. It takes a little girl with blue eyes and a spiked drink," my bodyguard sneered back. "If you think I'm going to let you live *that* one down...."

I forced myself to ignore them. While it was tempting to rally to Luanna's defense, there were other more pressing matters to attend to.

Moving as carefully as I could, I looped one end of the rope up and around Massha's waist. It took a couple of tries and a lot more rope than I would have liked, but finally I managed to catch the dangling end and tie it off securely.

"What's with the rope, Hot Stuff?" Massha said calmly, the only one of our group who had managed to keep her cool through the entire proceedings.

"Well, with any luck, in a little while we're going to be heading down...with Aahz," I explained. "Even though I know you're strong, I don't think your hands are strong enough to keep a grip on all three of us while we make the trip. This is to be sure we don't lose anyone *after* we spring the cell."

"Speaking of that," Aahz called, "I'm still waiting to hear how you're going to get me out of this thing. You might even say I'm *dying* to find out."

He wasn't the only one. The dragon's head was watching my every movement through slitted eyes. I'm not sure how much pride it took in its job, but it was obvious the beast wasn't getting ready to overwhelm us with its cooperation.

Everything was as ready as I could make it, so I decided it was time to play my trump card.

"There's nothing to it, really," I told my partner with a smile. "Talk to me."

It isn't often I catch my old mentor totally by surprise...I get him upset on a fairly regular basis, but total surprise was a real rarity. This was one of those golden times.

"Say WHAT?" Aahz exclaimed loudly.

"Trust me, Aahz," I insisted. "I know what I'm doing. Just talk to me. Tell me a story. How did you first meet

Garkin?'"

"Oh, that," he said, rolling his eyes expressively. "Well, we were at the same boring cocktail party, see... you know, one of those dreary affairs where the crowd has you pinned against the wall and you get stuck talking to whatever the tide washes up against you? Anyway, he was trying to impress some little bit of fluff with his magic, which really wasn't all that hot in those days...let me tell you, partner, anytime you start getting depressed with your lack of progress in the magic business, remind me to tell you what your old teacher Garkin was like when we first met. But, as I was saying, out of respect for the craft, I just had to wander over and show them what the *real* stuff looked like...not that I had any interest in her myself, mind you...."

I felt Guido tugging on my pantleg.

"Say, Boss," he complained. "What is this? I thought we were in a hurry."

"This is what we needed the time for," I whispered back.

"For *this?*" he grumbled. "But Boss, if we don't get started...."

"We're started," I answered. "Now pay attention to what he's saying."

I was afraid our side comments might have distracted Aahz, but I needn't have worried. As per normal, once my partner got on a verbal roll, he wasn't that easy to stop.

"...so there we were, just the three of us, mind you, and remember, our clothes were five floors away at this point...."

"What's going on, Hot Stuff?" Massha hissed from her position above me. "I *know* you've heard this story before. Heck, *I've* heard it four times myself."

"Keep your eye on the dragon," I advised her. "And be ready to act fast."

I was going through the motions of reacting to Aahz's story and fielding the impatient questions of my assistants as best I could, but my real attention was focused on the dragon's head. My strategy was already working. Aahz's droning account of past glories were starting to take effect.

The dragon's eyes were definitely starting to glaze.

"...of course, after all that, I just *had* to take her home with me. It was the least I could do for the poor thing under the circumstances."

Aahz was winding up his story already! I had to keep him going just a little bit longer.

"Was that the party where you met Tananda?" I said, deliberately feeding him another cue.

"Tananda? No. That's another story completely. I met her when I was sitting in on a cut-throat game of dragon poker over at the Geek's. We had a real pigeon on the line, the kind of idiot who would bet a busted Corp's a' Corp's into a Unicorn Flush showing, you know? Well, I was a little low on funds just then, so...."

Guido was getting restless again.

"Boss, how much longer are we gonna...."

"Not much longer," I interrupted. "Get hold of the rope. We're about to move."

"...now I was holding Ogres back-to-back...or was it Elves? No, it was Ogres. I remember because Tananda had Elves wrapped up. Of course, we didn't know that until the end of the hand. Anyway, as soon as the Geek opened, I bumped him back limit, and Tananda..."

That did it. I should have known a hand-by-hand, bet-by-bet description of dragon poker would do the trick.

Without any warning at all, the dragon yawned... long and wide.

Aahz broke off his narration, a momentous event in itself, and blinked his surprise.

"Quick, Aahz! Jump for it!"

Bewildered as he was, there was nothing wrong with my partner's reflexes. He was out of the dragon's mouth in a flash, diving through the air to catch the rope below

Guido.

As soon as his hands closed on our lifeline, several things happened at the same time.

With the extra weight on Massha's levitation belt, our whole formation started to sink at an alarming rate... my apprentice lost her grip on me, giving me minor rope burns as I clutched madly for the rope, almost too late to follow the advice I had been so freely giving to everyone else...and the dragon closed his mouth.

I caught one last glimpse of the beast before we sank from sight, and I honestly don't think he even knew we were gone. His eyelids were at half-mast, and the eyes themselves were out of focus from boredom. Aahz's stories tended to have that effect on even vaguely-intelligent beings. I had simply found a practical application for the phenomenon.

"I've gotta change the controls, Hot Stuff!" Massha called, alerting me once more to our current situation.

The ground was rushing up to meet us with frightening speed.

I remembered the faulty controls that held all of us at their mercy.

"No! Wait, Massha! Let me try...."

Exerting my last ounce of reserve power, I worked at levitating our whole crew. Under normal circumstances, I could lift three people easily and four or five in a pinch. Here in Limbo, using everything I had with Massha's belt assisting me, I barely managed to slow our descent to a moderate crawl.

"What happened there, partner?" Aahz called. "How did you know that thing was going to yawn?"

"Call it a lucky guess," I grunted, still concentrating on keeping us from crashing. "I'll explain later."

"Check the landing zone," Guido warned.

I sneaked a peak.

We had been at our task longer than I thought. The sidewalk below was crowded with vampires strolling here and there as Blut's legendary nightlife fired up.

"I don't think we can bluff our way through this one," Aahz said calmly. "Any chance you can steer us around the corner into the alley? There doesn't seem to be as much of a crowd there."

Before I could answer, something flashed past us from above with a flutter of leather wings.

"JAILBREAK!" it screamed, banking around the corner. "Murderer on the loose! JAILBREAK!"

# Chapter XIII

*"I've never seen
so damn many Indians."*
**G. A. Custer**

THE words of alarm had an interesting effect on the crowd below. After a brief glance to see us descending into their midst, to a man they turned and ran. In a twinkling, the street was empty.

"What's going on?" I called to Aahz, unable to believe our good fortune.

"Beats me!" my partner shouted back. "I guess none of the normal citizenry want to tangle with an escaped murderer. Better get us down fast before they figure out how badly outnumbered we are."

I didn't have to be told twice. Our escape had just gotten an unexpected blessing, but I wasn't about to make book on how long it would last. I cut my magical support, and we dropped swiftly toward the pavement.

"What was that that blew the whistle on us?" Massha said, peering up into the darkness where our mysterious saboteur had disappeared.

"I think it was that Vic character," Guido answered from below me. "I got a pretty good look at him when he bolted past me back at the Woof Writers."

"Really?" I asked, half to myself, twisting around to look after the departed villain. "That's one more we owe him."

"Later," Aahz commanded, touching down at last. "Right now we've got to get out of here."

Guido was beside him in a second. I had to drop a ways, as with the extra weight removed from the rope, we had ceased to sink.

"C'mon, Massha!" I called. "Cut the power in that thing. It's not that far to fall."

"I'm trying!" she snapped back, fiddling with the belt buckle once more. "The flaming thing's malfunctioning again!"

The belt setting had changed. Holding the rope, I could feel that there was no longer an upward pull. Unfortunately, Massha wasn't sinking, either. Instead, she hovered in mid-air about fifteen feet up.

"Hey, Boss! We got company!"

I followed by bodyguard's gaze. There was a mob forming down the street to our left, and it didn't look happy. Of course, it was hard to tell for sure, but I had the definite impression that their eyes were glowing redder than normal, which I was unable to convince myself was a good sign.

"Maasshhhha!" I nagged, my voice rising uncontrollably as I tugged on the rope.

"It's jammed!" she whimpered. "Go on, take off, Hot Stuff. No sense in all of us getting caught."

"We can't just leave you here," I argued.

"We don't have time for a debate," Aahz snarled. "Guido! Get up there ahead of us and keep the street open. We can't afford to get cut off. Okay, let's go!"

With that, he snatched the rope out of my hand and took off running down the street away from the crowd with Guido out front in point position and Massha floating over his head like a gaudy balloon. For once, I didn't object to him giving orders to my bodyguard. I was

112

too busy sprinting to keep up with the rest of my group.

If the watching mob was having any trouble deciding what to do, the sight of us fleeing settled it. With a howl, they swarmed down the street in pursuit.

When I say "with a howl," I'm not speaking figuratively. As they ran, some of the vampires transformed into large, fierce-looking dogs, others into bats, presumably to gain more speed in the chase. While Aahz and I had been chased by mobs before, this was the first pack of pursuers who literally bayed at our heels. I must say I didn't care much for the experience.

"Where are we going, Aahz?" I panted.

"Away from them!" he called back.

"I mean, eventually," I pressed. "We're heading the wrong way to get back to our hideout."

"We can't hole up until we've shaken our fan club," my partner insisted. "Now shut up and run."

I had certain doubts about our ability to elude our pursuers while towing Massha overhead to mark our position, but I followed Aahz's instructions and pumped the pavement for all I was worth. For one thing, if I pointed out this obvious fact to my partner, he might simply let go of the rope and leave my apprentice to fend for herself. Then again, the option to running was to stand firm and face the mob. All in all, running seemed like a *real* good idea.

Guido was surprisingly good at clearing a path for us. I had never really seen my bodyguard in action, but with his constant carping and allergy problems throughout this venture, I was tending to discount his usefulness. Not so. The vampires we encountered in our flight had not heard the alarm and were unprepared for the whirlwind that burst into their midst. Guido never seemed to break stride as he barreled into victim after victim, but whatever he did to them was effective. None of the fallen bodies which marked his progress attempted to interfere with Aahz or I...heck, they didn't even move.

"River ahead, Boss!" he called over his shoulder.

"What's that?" I puffed, realizing for the first time how out of shape I had grown during my prosperous stay at the Bazaar.

"A river!" he repeated. "The street we're on is going to dead-end into a river in a few blocks. I can see it from here. We're going to have to change direction or we'll get pinned against the water."

I wondered whether it wouldn't be a good idea for us to just plunge into the river and put some moving water between us and the vampires, as I seemed to recall a legend that that was one of the things that could stop them. Then it occurred to me that my bodyguard probably couldn't swim.

"Head right!" Aahz shouted. "There! Up that alley."

Guido darted off on the indicated course with my partner and I pounding along about fifteen paces behind him. We had built up a bit of a lead on our pursuers, though we could still hear their cries and yelps a block or so back, and for the first time I started to have the hope that we might actually elude them. Now that we were out of their line of sight....

"Look out...."

There was a sudden cry from above, and Massha came crashing to the ground, gaining the dubious distinction of being the first person I've ever witnessed doing a belly-flop on dry land. I'm sure the ground didn't actually shake, but the impact was enough to leave that impression. I experienced a quick flash of guilt, realizing that my first thought was not for the well-being of my apprentice, but rather unbridled relief that she hadn't landed on one of us.

"I think the controls just came unstuck," Aahz said, rather unnecessarily to my thinking.

"Are you all right, Massha?" I said, crouching over her.

"Wha—ha..." came the forced reply.

"Of course, she's not all right," Aahz snapped, assuming translator duties. "At the very least she's got the wind knocked out of her."

Whatever the exact extent of the damages were suffered from her fall, my apprentice wasn't even trying to rise. I would have liked to give her a few minutes recovery time, but already the sounds of our pursuers were drawing closer.

"Can you carry her, Aahz?"

"Not on my best day," my partner admitted, eyeing Massha's sizable bulk. "How about you? Have you got enough juice left to levitate her?"

I shook my head violently.

"Used it all supervising our aerial maneuvers back at the jail."

"Hey, Boss!" Guido hissed, emerging from the shadows behind us. "The alley's blocked. This is the only way out!"

And that was that. Even if we got Massha up and moving, all it meant was that we'd have to retrace our steps right back into the teeth of the mob. We had run our race . . . and were about to lose it rather spectacularly.

The others knew it, too.

"Well, it's been nice working with you, Guido," Aahz said with a sigh. "I know I've gotten on your case a couple of times, but you're a good man to have around in a pinch. You did some really nice crowd work getting us this far. Sorry about that last turn call."

"No hard feelings," my bodyguard shrugged. "You gave it your best shot. This alley would have been my choice, too, if I'd been workin' alone. Boss, I warned you I was a jinx when it came to jailbreaks. I gotta admit, though, for a while there I really thought we were goin' to pull this one off."

"It was a long shot at best." I grinned. "At least you can't say that *this* one suffered from over-planning."

Aahz clapped a hand on my shoulder.

"Well, partner?" he said. "Any thoughts on how to play this one? Do we try to surrender peacefully, or go down swinging?"

I wasn't sure the crowd would give us a choice. They were almost at our alley, and they didn't sound like they cared much for talking.

"NOT THIS WAY! THEY'RE DOUBLING BACK TOWARD THE JAIL!"

This unexpected cry came from the street near the mouth of our alley.

I couldn't believe it, but apparently the mob did. There were curses and shouted orders, but from their fast-fading manner it was plain that the crowd had turned and was now heading back the way they had come.

"What was that?" Massha managed, her voice returning at last.

I motioned her to be silent and cocked an eyebrow at Aahz, silently asking the same question.

He answered with an equally silent shake of the head.

Neither of us knew for sure what was going on, but we both sensed that the timely intervention was neither accidental nor a mistake. Someone had deliberately pulled the crowd off our backs. Before we celebrated our good fortune, we wanted to know who and why.

A pair of figures appeared at the mouth of the alley.

"You can come out now," one of them called. 'Sorry to interfere, but it looked like so much fun we just *had* to play, too."

I'd know that voice anywhere, even if I didn't recognize the figure as well as the unmistakable form of her brother.

"Tananda! Chumley!" I shouted, waving to pinpoint our position. "I was wondering when you'd show up."

The sister-brother team of Trollop and Troll hastened to join us. For all their lighthearted banter, I can think of few beings I'd rather have on or at my side when things get tight.

"Are you all right?" Tananda asked, stopping to help Massha to her feet.

"Really never had much dignity," my apprentice responded, "and what little I did have is shot to hell. Except for that I'm fine. I'm starting to see why you Big Leaguers are so down on mechanical magic."

Chumley seized my hand and pumped it vigorously.

"Now don't be too rough on your little gimmicks, ducks," he advised. "That little ring you left us was just the ticket we needed to get here in time for the latest in our unbroken string of last-minute rescues. Except for the typical hash you've made of your end-game, it looks like you've all done rather well without us. We've got all present and accounted for, including Aahz, who seems remarkably unscathed after yet one more near-brush with disaster. Seems like all that's left is a hasty retreat and a slow celebration...eh, what?"

"That's about the size of it," I agreed. "It's great having the two of you along to ride shotgun on our exit, though. Speaking of which, can you find the castle from here? I've gotten a little turned around...."

"Hold it right there!" Aahz broke in. "Before we get too wrapped up in congratulating each other, aren't there a few minor details being overlooked?"

The group looked at each other.

"Like what?" Tananda said at last.

"Like the fact that I'm still wanted for murder, for one," my partner glared. "Then again, there's the three fugitives we're supposed to be bringing back to Deva with us."

"Oh, come on, Aahz," the Trollop chided, poking him playfully in the ribs. "With the reputation you already have, what's a little thing like a murder warrant?"

"I didn't do it," Aahz insisted. "Not only didn't I kill this Vic character, nobody did. He's still around somewhere laughing down his sleeve at all of us. Now while I'll admit my reputation isn't exactly spotless, it doesn't include standing still for a bum rap. . .or letting someone get away with making a fool of me!"

"Of course, saving the money for paying the swindlers' debts plus the fines involved has nothing to do with it, eh, Aahz?" Chumley said, winking his larger eye.

"Well. . .that, too," my partner admitted. "Isn't it nice that we can take care of both unpleasant tasks at the same time?"

"Maybe we could settle for just catching Vic and let the others go," I murmured.

"How's that again, partner?"

"Nothing, Aahz," I said with a sigh. "It's just that. . .nothing. C'mon everybody. If we're going to go hunting, it's going to require a bit of planning, and I don't think we should do it out here in the open."

# Chapter XIV

*"Relax, Julie.*
*Everyone will understand."*
**Romeo**

FORTUNATELY, Massha's elevated position during our flight had given her an excellent view of our surroundings, and we were able to find our way back to the Dispatcher's without being discovered by the aroused populace. Now that our numbers had increased, however, Vilhelm's greeting was noticeably cooler.

"I'm starting to believe what everybody says," the little vampire complained. "Let one demon in, and the next thing you know the neighborhood's crawling with them. When I decided to talk to you folks instead of blowing the whistle on you, I didn't figure on turning my office into a meeting place for off-worlders."

"C'mon, Vilhelm," I said, trying to edge my foot into the doorway. "We don't have any place else to go in town. There aren't *that* many of us."

"We could always just wait out on the street until the authorities come by," Aahz suggested. "I don't imagine it would take much to convince them that this guy has been harboring fugitives."

"Can it, Green and Scaly," Massha ordered, puffing

herself up to twice her normal size. "Vilhelm's been nice to us so far, and I won't listen to anyone threaten him, even you. Just remember that you'd still be cooling your heels in the slammer if it weren't for him. Either he helps of his own free will, or we look elsewhere."

Aahz gave ground before her righteous indignation.

"Are you going to let your apprentice talk to me that way?" he demanded.

"Only when she's right." I shrugged.

"I say, Aahz," Chumley intervened. "Could you possibly curb your normally vile manners for a few moments? We don't really need one more enemy in this dimension, and I, for one, would appreciate the chance to extend my thanks to this gentleman before he throws us out."

When he's working, Chumley goes by the name of Big Crunch and does a Neanderthal that's the envy of half the barbarians at the Bazaar. On his own time, however, his polished charm has solved a lot of problems for us... almost as many as Aahz's bluster has gotten us into.

"Oh, come on in," the Dispatcher grumbled. "Enter freely and of your own accord and all that. I never could turn my back on somebody in trouble. Guess that's why I've never traveled the other dimensions myself. They'd eat me alive out there."

"Thanks, Vilhelm," I said, slipping past him into the office before he could change his mind. "You'll have to forgive my partner. He really isn't always like this. Being on death row hasn't done much for his sense of humor."

"I guess I'm a little edgy myself," the vampire admitted. "Strange as it sounds, I've been worried about you folks...and your motor-mouthed friend who's been keeping me company hasn't helped things much."

I did a quick nose count of our troop.

"Wait a minute," I frowned. "Who's been waiting for us?"

Now it was Vilhelm's turn to look surprised.

"Didn't one of you send out for a werewolf? He said he

was with you."

"Aahh! But I am! My friends, they do not know me yet, but I shall be their salvation, no?"

With that, I was overwhelmed by a shaggy rug. Well, at least that's what I thought until it came off the floor and threw itself into my arms with the enthusiasm of a puppy...a very large puppy.

"What's *that*?!" Aahz said, his eyes narrowing dangerously. "Skeeve, can't I leave you alone for a few days without you picking up every stray in any given dimension?"

"That," in this case, was one of the scroffiest-looking werewolves I'd ever seen...realizing, of course, that until this moment I'd only seen two. He had dark bushy eyebrows (if you'll belive that on a werewolf) and wore a white stocking cap with a maple leaf on the side. His whiskers were carefully groomed into a handlebar mustache, and what might have been a goatee peered from beneath his chin. Actually, viewed piecemeal, he was very well-groomed. It's just when taken in its entirety that he looked scroffy. Maybe it was the leer....

"Honest, Aahz," I protested, trying to untangle myself. "I've never seen him before in my life!"

"Oh, but forgive me," the beast said, releasing me so suddenly I almost fell. "I am so stupeed, I forget to introduce. So! I am an artist extraordinaire, but also, I am ze finest track-air in ze land. My friends, the Woof Writers, they have told me of your pro-blem and I have flown like ze wind to aid you. No? I am Pepe Le Garou A. and I am at your service."

With that, he swept into a low bow with a flourish that if I hadn't been so flabbergasted I would have applauded. It occurred to me that now I knew why the Woof Writers had snickered when they told us they knew of someone who could help.

"Boss," Guido said, his voice muffled by his hand, which he was holding over his nose and mouth. "Shall I wait outside?"

Tananda cocked an eyebrow at him.

"Allergy problems? Here, try some of this. No dimension traveler should be without it."

She produced a small vial and tossed it to my bodyguard. "Rub some onto your upper lip just below your nose."

"Gee, thanks," Guido said, following her instructions. "What is it?"

"It's a counter-allergenic paste." She shrugged. "I think it has a garlic base."

"WHAT?" my bodyguard exclaimed, dropping the vial.

Tananda favored him with one of her impish grins.

"Just kidding. Nunzio was worried about you and told us about your allergies...all of them."

Her brother swatted her lightly on the rump.

"Shame on you, little sister," he said, smiling in spite of himself. "After you get done apologizing to Guido, I suggest you do the same for our host. I think you nearly have him a heart attack with that last little joke."

This was, of course, just what I needed while stranded in a hostile dimension. A nervous vampire, a melodramatic werewolf, and now my teammates decide it's time to play practical jokes on each other.

"Ummm...tell me, Mr. A.," I said, ignoring my other problems and turning to the werewolf. "Do you think you can...."

"No, non," he interrupted. "Eet is simply Pepe, eh?"

"Pepe A.," I repeated dutifully.

"Zat's right," he beamed, apparently delighted with my ability to learn a simple phrase. "Now, before we... how you say, get down to ze business, would you do me ze hon-air of introducing me to your colleagues?"

"Oh. Sorry. This is my partner, Aahz. He's...."

"But of course! Ze famous Aahz! I have so long wished to meet you."

# Pepe Le Garou A.

If there's anything that can coax Aahz out of a bad mood, it's flattery...and Pepe seemed to be an expert in that category.

"You've heard of me?" he blinked. "I mean...what exactly have you heard? There have been so many adventures over the years."

"Do you not remem-bair Piere? I was raised from a pup on his tales of your fight with Isstvan."

"Piere? You know Piere?"

"Do I know him? He is my uncle!"

"No kidding. Hey, Tananda! Did you hear that? Pepe here's Piere's nephew. Wait'll we tell Gus."

I retired from the conversation, apparently forgotten in the reunion.

"Say, Skeeve," Vilhelm said, appearing at my side. "It looks like this could take a while. Should I break out the wine?"

That got my attention.

"Wine? You've got wine?"

"Stocked up on it after your last visit," the vampire admitted with a grin. "Figured it might come in handy the next time you came through. I may gripe a bit, but talking to you and your friends is a lot more fun than watching the tubes."

"Well bring it out...but I get the first glass. Unless you've got lots there won't be much left after my partner there gets his claws on it."

I turned back to the proceedings just in time to see Pepe kissing my apprentice's hand.

"Do not be afraid, my little flow-air," he was saying. "Here is one who truly appreciates your beauty, as well as...how should I say it, its quantity?"

"You're kinda cute," Massha giggled. "But I never did go in much for inter-species dating, if you get my drift."

I caught Aahz's attention and drew him away from the group.

"Could you take over for a while here, partner?" I

said. "I've been running nonstop since the start of this thing and could use a little time by myself to recharge my batteries before we fire up again."

"No problem," he nodded, laying a hand on my shoulder. "I figure we won't be moving before sun-up...and Skeeve? I haven't had a chance to say it, but thanks for the bail-out."

"Don't mention it," I grinned weakly. "Tell me you wouldn't do the same for me."

"Don't know," he retorted. "You've never sucker-punched me at the beginning of a caper."

"Now *that* I still owe you for."

Just then, Vilhelm appeared with the wine, and Aahz hurried away to rejoin the group.

I managed to snag a goblet and retired to a secluded corner while the party went into high gear. Pepe seemed to be fitting in well with the rest of the team, if not functioning as a combination jester and spark plug, but somehow I felt a bit distant. Sipping my wine, I stared off into the distance at nothing in particular, letting my thoughts wander.

"What's the trouble, handsome?"

"Hmmm? Oh. Hi, Tananda. Nothing in particular. Just a little tired, that's all."

"Mind if I join you?" she said, dropping to the floor beside me before I could stop her. "So. Are you going to tell me about it? Who is she?"

I turned my head slowly to look at her directly.

"I beg your pardon?"

She kept her eyes averted, idly running one finger around the rim of her goblet.

"Look," she said, "if you don't want to talk about it, just say so...it's really none of my business. Just don't try to kid me or yourself that there's nothing bothering you. I've known you a long time now, and I can usually tell when there's something eating you. My best guess right now, if I'm any judge of the phenomenon, is that it's a girl."

Ever since I'd met Tananda, I'd had a crush on her. With her words, though, I suddenly realized how badly I wanted someone to talk to. I mean, to Guido and Massha I was an authority figure, and I wasn't about to open up to Aahz until I was sure he'd take the problem seriously and not just laugh, and as for Chumley...how do you talk about woman problems with a troll?

"Okay. You got me," I said, looking back into my wine. "It's a girl."

"I thought so," Tananda smiled. "Where have you been keeping her? Tell me, is she beautiful and sensitive?"

"All that and more." I nodded, taking another drink from my goblet. "She's also on the wrong side."

"Woops," Tananda said, straightening up. "You'd better run that one past me again."

I filled her in on my encounters with Luanna. I tried to keep it unbiased and informative, but even I could tell that my tones were less controlled than I would have liked.

Tananda sat in silence for a few moments after I'd finished, hugging her legs and with her chin propped up on her knees.

"Well," she said at last, "from what you say, she's an accomplice at best. Maybe we can let her go after we get them all rounded up."

"Sure."

My voice was flat. Both Tananda and I knew that once Aahz got on his high horse there was no telling how merciful or vicious he would be at any given point.

"Well, there's always a chance," she insisted. "Aahz has always had a soft spot where you're concerned. If you intercede for her, and if she's willing to abandon her partners...."

"...and, if a table had wings, we could fly it back to the Bazaar." I frowned. "No, Tananda. First of all, she won't give up her partners just because they're in a crunch. That much I know. Besides, if I put that kind of pressure on her, to choose between me and them, I'd never

126

know for sure if she really wanted me or if she was just trying to save her own skin."

Tananda got to her feet.

"Don't become so wise that you're stupid, Skeeve," she said softly before she left. "Remember, Luanna's already chosen you twice over her partners. Both times she's risked her life and their getaway to pass you a warning. Maybe all she needs is what you haven't yet given her—an invitation for a chance at a new life with a new partner. Don't be so proud or insecure that you'd throw a genuine admirer to the wolves rather than run the risk of making a mistake. If you did, I don't think I'd like you much...and I don't think you would either."

I pondered Tananda's advice after she'd gone. There was one additional complication I hadn't had the nerve to mention to her. Whatever Luanna's feelings for me were, how would they change when she found out I'd used her scarf...her token of affection, to guide a pack of hunters to their target?

# Chapter XV

*"Everybody needs
a career manager!"*
**Lady Macbeth**

So where is he?" Aahz grumbled for the hundredth time. . .in the last five minutes.

The sun had been up for hours, or at least as up as it seemed to get in this dimension. Since my arrival in Limbo, I had never seen what I am accustomed to thinking of as full sunlight. Whether the constant heavy overcast condition which seemed to prevail during daylight hours was the result of magic or some strange meteorologic condition I was never sure, but it did nothing to alleviate the air of gloom that clung to the town of Blut like a shroud.

The whole team was impatient to get started, but Aahz was the only one who indulged himself in expressing his feelings as often. . .or as loudly. Of course, it might have been simply that he was making so much of a fuss that the others were willing to let him provide the noise for all of them rather than letting their own efforts get constantly upstaged.

"Just take it easy, partner," I said soothingly, struggling to keep from snapping at him in my own nervous impatience. "There aren't that many all-day stores in this dimension."

"What do you expect, dealing with a bunch of vampires," he snapped. "I still don't like this idea. Nonmagical disguises seem unnatural somehow."

I heaved a quiet sigh inside and leaned back to wait, propping my feet up on a chair. This particular quarrel was old before Vilhelm had left on his shopping trip, and I was tired going over it again and again.

"Be reasonable, Aahz," Tananda said, taking up the slack for me. "You know we can't wander around town like this...especially you with half the city looking for you. We need disguises, and without a decent power source, Skeeve here can't handle disguises for all of us. Besides, it's not like we're using mechanical magic. We won't be using magic at all."

"That's what everybody keeps telling me," my partner growled. "We're just going to alter our appearances without using spells. That sounds like mechanical magic to me. Do you know what's going to happen to our reputations if word of this gets back to the Bazaar? Particularly with most of the competition looking for a chance to splash a little mud on the Great Skeeve's name? Remember, we're already getting complaints that our prices are too high, and if this gets out...."

The light dawned. I could finally see what was eating at Aahz. I should have known there was money at the bottom of this.

"But Aahz," I chimed in, "our fees *are* overpriced. I've been saying that for months. I mean, it's not like we need the money...."

"...and I've been telling you for months that it's the only way to keep the riff-raff from draining away all your practice time," he shot back angrily. "Remember, your name's supposed to be the Great Skeeve, not the Red Cross. You don't do charity."

Now we were on familiar ground. Unlike the disguise

thing, this was one argument I never tired of.

"I'm not talking about charity," I said. "I'm talking about a fair fee for services rendered."

"Fair fee?" my partner laughed, rolling his eyes. "You mean like that deal you cut with Watzisname? Did he ever tell you about that one, Tananda? We catch a silly bird for this Deveel, see, and my partner charges him a flat fee. Not a percentage, mind you, a flat fee. And how much of a flat fee? A hundred gold pieces? A thousand. No. TEN. Ten lousy gold pieces. And half an hour later the Deveel sells his 'poor little bird' for over a hundred thousand. Nice to know we don't do charity, isn't it?"

"C'mon, Aahz," I argued, writhing inside. "That was only five minutes' work. How was I supposed to know the silly bird was on the endangered species list? Even *you* thought it was a good deal until we heard what the final sale was. Besides, if I had held out for a percentage and the Deveel had been legit and never sold the thing, we wouldn't have even gotten ten gold pieces out of it."

"I never heard the details from your side," Tananda said, "but what I picked up on the streets that everybody at the Bazaar was really impressed. Most folks think that it's a master-stroke of PR for the hottest magician at the Bazaar to help bring a rarity to the public for a mere fraction of his normal fees. It shows he's something other than a cold-hearted businessman...that he really cares about people."

"So what's wrong with being a cold-hearted business-man?" Aahz snorted. "How about the other guy? Every-body thinks he's a villain, and he's crying all the way to the bank. He retired on the profit from that one sale alone."

"Unless Nanny misled me horribly when she taught me my numbers," Chumley interrupted, "I figure your current bankroll could eat that fellow's profit and still have room for lunch. Any reason you're so big on squir-reling away so much gold, Aahz? Are you planning on retiring?"

130

"No, I'm not planning on retiring," my partner snapped. "And you're missing the point completely. Money isn't the object."

"It isn't?"

I think everybody grabbed that line at the same time...even Pepe, who hadn't known Aahz all that long.

"Of course not. You can always get more gold. What can't be replaced is time. We all know Skeeve here has a long way to go in the magic department. What the rest of you keep forgetting is how short a life span he has to play with...maybe a hundred years if he's lucky. All I'm trying to do is get him the maximum learning time possible...and that means keeping him from using up most of his time on nickel-and-dime adventures. Let the small-time operators do those. My partner shouldn't have to budge away from his studies unless the assignment is something *really* spectacular. Something that will advance his reputation and his career."

There was a long silence while everybody digested that one, especially me. Since Aahz had accepted me as a full partner instead of an apprentice, I tended to forget his role as my teacher and career manager. Thinking back now, I could see he had never really given up the work, just gotten sneakier. I wouldn't have believed that was possible.

"How about this particular nickel-and-dime adventure?" Tananda said, breaking the silence. "You know, pulling your tail out of a scrape? Isn't this a little low-brow for the kind of legend you're trying to build?"

The sarcasm in her voice was unmistakable, but it didn't phase Aahz in the least.

"If you'll ask around, you'll find out that I didn't want him along on this jaunt at all. In fact, I knocked him cold trying to keep him out. A top-flight magician shouldn't have to stoop to bill collecting, especially when the risk is disproportionately high."

"Well, it all sounds a little cold-blooded for my taste,

Aahz," Chumley put in. "If you extend your logic, our young friend here is only going to work when the danger is astronomically high, and conversely if the advancement to his career is enough, no risk is too great. That sounds to me like a sure-fire way to lose a partner *and* a friend. Like the Geek says, if you keep bucking the odds, sooner or later they're going to catch up with you."

My partner spun to confront the troll nose-to-nose.

"Of course it's going to be dangerous," he snarled. "The magic profession isn't for the faint of heart, and to hit the top he's going to have to be hair-triggered and mean. There's no avoiding that, but I can try to be sure he's ready for it. Why do you think I've been so dead-set against him having bodyguards? If he starts relying on other people to watch out for him, he's going to lose the edge himself. *That's* when he's in danger of walking into a swinging door.

That brought Guido into the fray.

"Now let me see if I've got this right," my bodyguard said. "You don't want me and my cousin Nunzio around so that the Boss here can handle all the trouble himself? That's crazy talk, know what I mean? Now listen to me, 'cause this time I know what I'm sayin'. The higher someone gets on the ladder, the more folks come huntin' for his head. Even if they don't do nothin' they got people gunning for them, 'cause they got power and respect and there's always somebody who thinks they can steal it. Now I've seen some of the Big Guys who try to act just like you're sayin'. . . they're so scared all the time they don't trust nothin' or nobody. The only one they can count on is themselves, and everybody else is suspect. That includes total strangers, their own bodyguards, their friends, *and* their partners. Think about *that* for a minute."

He leaned back and surveyed the room, addressing his next comments to everyone.

"People like that don't last long. They don't trust nobody, so they got nobody. Ya can't do everything alone, and sooner or later they're lookin' the wrong way or asleep when they should be watchin' and it's all over. Now I've done a lot of jobs as a bodyguard, and they were just jobs, know what I mean? The Boss here is different, and I'm not just sayin' that. He's the best man I've met in my whole life because he likes people and ain't afraid to show it. More important, he ain't afraid to risk his neck to help somebody even if it *isn't* in his best interest. I work double hard for him because I don't want to see anything happen to him...and if that means comin' along on weird trips like this, then that's the way it is. Anybody that wants to hurt him is gonna have to come through me...and that includes fightin' any of you if you want to try to turn him into somethin' he isn't and doesn't want to be."

Massha broke in with a loud clapping of her hands.

"Bravo, Guido," she said. "I think your problem, Green and Scaly, is that your idea of success is out of step with everyone else's. We all want to see good things happen for Skeeve, here, but we also like him just the way he is. We've got enough faith in his good sense to back him in whatever move he makes in his development...without trying to frog-march or trick him up a specific path."

Aahz not only gave ground before this onslaught of protest, he seemed to shrink in a little on himself.

"I like him too," he mumbled. "I've known him longer than any of you, remember? He's doing fine, but he could be so much more. How can he choose a path if he can't see it? All I'm trying to do is set him up to be bigger than I...than *we* could ever think of being ourselves. What's wrong with that?"

Despite my irritation at having my life discussed as if I weren't in the room, I was quite touched, by my friends' loyal defense of me, and most of all by Aahz.

"You know, partner," I said softly, "for a minute there, you sounded just like my father. He wanted me to be the best...or more specifically, to be better than he was. My mom always tried to tell me that it was because

133

he loved me, but at that time it just sounded like he was always being critical. Maybe she was right...I'm more inclined to believe it today than I was then, but then again, I'm older now. If nothing else, I've had to try to tell peple I love them when the words just won't come...and gotten upset with myself when they couldn't see it when I tried to show them.

"Aahz, I appreciate your concern and I want your guidance. You're right, there are paths and options I can't even comprehend yet. But I also have to choose my own way. I want to be better eventually than I am today, but not necessarily the best. I think Guido's right, there's a big price tag attached to being at the top, and I'd want to think long and hard if I wanted to pay it...even if I was convinced I could, which I'm not. I *do* know that if it means giving up the trust I have in you and everybody else in this room, I'll settle for being a nickel-and-dime operator. *That* price I'll never pay willingly."

Silence started to descend again as each of us retreated into his or her own thoughts, then the werewolf bounded into the middle of the assemblage.

"But what is this, eh?" he demanded. "Surely this cannot be ze great team of Aahz and Skeeve, ze ones who can laugh at any dan-gair?"

"You know, Pepe," Aahz said warningly, "you've got a great future as a stuffed head."

"My head?" The werewolf blinked. "But she is not...oohh. I see now. You make ze joke, eh? Good. Zat is more like it."

"...and as far as laughing at danger goes," I joined in, determined to hold up my end of the legend, "the only danger I see here is dying of boredom. Where *is* Vilhelm anyway?"

"I know you and Aahz are fond of each other, Skeeve," Chumley yawned, "but you've *got* to spend more time with other people. You're starting to sound like him. Maybe you can tag along the next time I have an assignment."

"Over my dead body," my partner said. "Besides, what could he learn from a troll that I couldn't teach him myself?"

"I could teach him not to catch birds for Deveels for ten gold pieces," the troll grinned, winking at his sister. "That seems to be a part of his education you've neglected."

"Izzat so!" my partner bristled. "You're going to teach him about price setting? How about the time you set your own sister up to steal an elephant without bothering to check. . . ."

And they were off again. As I listened, I found myself reflecting on the fact that while it was nice to know the depths of my friends' feelings about me, it was far more comfortable when they managed to conceal it under a cloak of banter. For the most part, open sincerity is harder to take than friendly laughter.

# Chapter XVI

*"Don't be fooled by appearances."*
**Malloy**

THINGS were pretty much back to normal by the time Vilhelm returned with our disguises . . . which was a good thing as the process of masking-up proved to be a test of everybody's sense of humor.

Until I had hooked up with Aahz, I had never had occasion to pretend I was anyone but myself. As such, I had no way of knowing how long it took to don a physical disguise without resorting to magic. By the time we were done, I had a new respect for the skills I had learned, not to mention a real longing for a dimension . . . any dimension with a strong force line to work with.

Tananda was a major help, her experiences with the assassin's guild came into play and she took the lead in trying to coach us into our new roles.

"Guido, straighten up!" she commanded, exasperation creeping into her voice. "You walk like a gangster."

"I am a gangster!" my bodyguard snarled back. "Besides, what's wrong with the way I walk? It got us to the jail, didn't it?"

"Half the town wasn't looking for you then," Tananda argued. "Besides, then you could pick your own route. We don't know where the opposition's holed up. We're going to have to walk through crowds on this hunt, and that walk just doesn't make it. Ninety percent of costuming is learning to move like the character you're trying to portray. Right now you move like you're looking for a fight."

"Try walking like Don Bruce," I suggested. "He's a gangster, too."

That earned me a black look, but my bodyguard tried to follow my instructions, rising up on the balls of his feet and mincing along.

"Better," Tananda said, leaving Guido prancing up and down the room with a scowl on his face.

"How are we doing?"

"Lousy," she confided in me. "This is taking a lot longer than it should. I wish there were more mirrors in this place...heck, any mirrors would be nice."

It hadn't been until we started gearing up that we realized the Dispatcher had no mirrors at all. He claimed they weren't popular or necessary among vampires. This left us with the unenviable job of checking each others' make-up and costumes, a chore which would have been Homeric even if less sensitive egos were involved.

"How're my teeth?" Massha demanded, sticking her head in front of me and opening her mouth.

It was like staring into the depths of an underground cave.

"Umm...the left side is okay, but you're still missing a few on the right. Hang on a second and I'll give you a hand."

Teeth were turning out to be a special problem. We had hoped to find some of the rubber fangs so prevalent in the Bazaar novelty stores to aid in our disguises. Unfortunately, none of the shops in Blut had them. The closest thing they had in stock, according to Vilhelm, were rubber sets of human teeth designed to fit over fangs. The vampire assured us that locally they were considered quite frightening. Faced by this unforeseen shortage, we were resorting to using tooth-black to blacken all our teeth except the canines for a close approximation of the vampires we were trying to imitate. When we tried it out, it wasn't a bad effect, but the actual application was causing countless problems. When one tried to apply the stuff on oneself without a mirror, it was difficult to get the right teeth, and if one called on one's friends for assistance, one rapidly found that said friend was soon possessed by an overpowering impulse to paint one's tongue black instead of the teeth.

"I don't like this cloak," Guido announced, grabbing my arm. "I want to wear my trench coat."

"Vampires don't wear trench coats," I said firmly. "Besides, the cloak really looks great on you. Makes you look. . . I don't know, debonair but menacing."

"Yeah?" he retorted skeptically, craning his neck to try to see himself.

"You think you've got problems?" Massha burst in. "Look at what I'm supposed to wear! I'll trade your cloak for this rig any day."

As you might have noticed, the team was having more than a little difficulty adapting to their disguises. Massha in particular was rebelling against her costume.

After having been floated over our escape like a balloon over a parade, we feared that she would be one of the most immediately recognizable of our group. As such, we not only dyed her garish orange hair, we insisted that her new costume cover as much of her as possible. To this end, Vilhelm had found a dress he called a "moo-moo," a name which did nothing toward endearing the garment to my apprentice.

"I mean, *really,* High Roller," she said, backing me toward a corner. "Isn't it bad enough that half the town's seen me as a blimp? Tell me I don't have to be a *cow* now."

"Honest, Massha," Vilhelm put in. "The style is fairly popular here in Blut. A lot of the ladies wear it who are... that is, are a bit...."

"Fat!?"

She loomed over the little vampire.

"Is that the word you're groping for, Short and About To Become Extinct?"

"Let's face it, dear," Tananda said, coming to the rescue. "You *are* carrying a little extra weight there. Believe me, if there's one time you can't kid yourself about your body, it's when you're donning costumes. If anything, that outfit makes you look a little slimmer."

"Don't try to kid a kidder, sweetie," Massha sighed. "But you're right about the costuming thing. This thing is so *drab,* though. First I'm a blimp, and now I'm an army tent."

"Now *that* I'll agree with," Tananda nodded. "Trust a man to find a drab mu-mu. Tell you what. There's a scarf I was going to use for a belt, but maybe you could wear it around your neck."

I was afraid that last crack would touch off another explosion, but Massha took it as a helpful suggestion and the two of them went off in search of other possible adornments.

"Got a minute, partner?"

From the tone of Aahz's voice, I knew the moment I had been dreading had arrived.

Chumley didn't have to worry about a disguise at all, as trolls were not uncommon in this dimension. Tananda also insisted that she looked enough like a vampire to pass with only minimal modifications. I hadn't seen any vampires with green hair, but she claimed that she had, so, as always, I yielded to her greater experience in these matters. I was also on the "minimal disguise" list, everyone agreeing that no one in Blut had gotten enough of a look at me to fix the image in their mind. While I wasn't wild about being so unmemorable, I went along with it... especially when I saw what Guido and Massha were going through. The problems with those two notables have already been mentioned: troublesome, but not insurmountable. Then there was Aahz. . . .

"Is there something wrong?" I asked innocently.

"You bet your dragon there's something wrong!" my partner snarled. "And don't try to play innocent with me! It didn't work when you were my apprentice, and it sure isn't going to work now."

Aahz's disguise had presented us with some knotty problems. Not only was he the most wanted member of our party, he was also easily the most distinctive. After the trial and his time in jail, it was doubtful that there was a single citizen of Blut who wouldn't recognize him on sight. I mean, there just aren't that many scaly green demons wandering around any dimension. . .except possibly his home dimension of Perv. It was therefore decided. . .almost unanimously. . .that not only would we change my partner's color with make-up, but that it would also be necessary to change his sex.

"Does this, perchance, have something to do with your disguise?" I inquired, trying to keep a straight face.

"Yes, it has something to do with my disguise," he mimicked, "and, so help me, partner or no, if you let that smile get away, I'll punch your lights out. Understand?"

With a great effort I sucked my cheeks in and bit my lower lip.

"Seriously, though," he said, almost pleading, "a joke's a joke, but you don't really expect me to go out in public looking like *this,* do you?"

In addition to the aforementioned make-up, Aahz's disguise required a dress and a wig. Because of the size of his head (a problem Vilhelm had wisely down-played as much as possible) the selection of wigs available had been understandably small. In fact, the only available in his size was a number called "Lady Go-GoDiva," which involved a high blonde beehive style offset by a long ponytail that hung down to his knees. Actually, the ponytail turned out to be a blessing in disguise, as the dark blue dress Vilhelm had selected for my partner turned out to have an exceptionally low neckline, and the hair draped over his shoulder helped hide the problem we had had finding ample or suitable material to stuff his bosom with.

"As my wise old mentor once told me when I was faced with a similar dilemma," I said sagely, "what does it matter what people think of you? They aren't supposed to know it's you, anyway. That's the whole idea of a disguise."

"But this get-up is humiliating!"

"My words precisely when someone else I could name deemed it necessary for *me* to dress up as a girl, remember?"

"You're enjoying this, aren't you?" Aahz glowered, peering at me suspiciously.

"Well, there are a couple of other options," I admitted.

"That's more like it!" he grinned, reaching for his wig.

"You could stay behind...."

His hand stopped just short of its mission.

"...or we could forget the whole thing and pay the fine ourselves."

The hand retreated as my partner's shoulders sagged in defeat. I felt no joy at the victory. If anything, I had been half hoping he would be embarrassed enough to take me up on my suggestion of abandoning the project. I should have known better. When there's money involved, it takes more than embarrassment to throw Aahz off the scent... whether the embarrassment is his own or someone else's.

"All right, everybody," I called, hiding my disappointment. "Are we ready to go?"

"Remember your sunglasses!" Tananda added.

That was the final touch to our disguises. To hide our non-red eyes, each of us donned a pair of sunglasses. Surveying the final result, I had to admit that aside from Tananda and Chumley, we didn't look like us. Exactly what we *did* look like I wouldn't venture to say, but we sure didn't look like *us*!

"Okay," Aahz chimed in, his discomfort apparently behind him. "Does everyone have their marching orders? Vilhelm? Are you sure you can track us on that thing?"

"No problem," the little vampire nodded. "When things get slow around here I use this rig to do a little window peeking right here in town. Covering the streets is even easier."

"Remember," I told him, "watch for our signal. When we catch up with this Vic character, we're going to want you to get some responsible local witnesses there chop-chop."

"Well now," Aahz grinned evilly, "you don't have to be *too* quick about it. I wouldn't mind having a little time alone with him before we turn him over to the authorities."

My heart sank a little. Aahz sounded determined to exact a bit of vengeance out of this hunt, and I wasn't at all sure he would restrict himself to Vic when it came time to express his ire.

I think Tananda noticed my concern.

"Ease up a little, Aahz," she said casually. "I don't mind helping you out of a tight spot, but count me out when it comes to excessive force for the sake of vengeance. It lacks class."

"Since when did you worry about excessive violence?" Aahz growled, then shrugged his acceptance. "Okay. But maybe we'll get lucky. Maybe he'll resist arrest."

I was still worried, but realized that that was about the most restraint I would get out of my partner.

"Now that that's settled," I said, producing Luanna's scarf, "Pepe, take a whiff of this."

"Enchanting," he smiled, nuzzling the piece of cloth. "A young lady, no? Eef ze body is as good as ze aroma, I will follow her to the end of ze world whether you accompany me or not."

I resisted an impulse to wrap the scarf around his

142

neck and pull.

"All right, everybody," I said, retrieving the scarf and tucking it back into my tunic in what I hoped was a casual manner. "Let's go catch us a renegade vampire."

# Chapter XVII

*"The trail's got to be
'round here somewhere!"*

**D. Boone**

IT was only a few hours short of sunset as we set out on our quest, a nagging reminder of exactly how long our efforts at physical disguise had taken. We had agreed to avoid following Pepe as a group so as not to attract attention. Instead, we moved singly or in groups of two, using both sides of the street and deliberately walking at different paces. The faster walkers averaged their progress with the slower by occasionally stopping to look into shop windows, thereby keeping our group together without actually appearing to. Tananda pointed out that not only would this procedure lessen our chances of being noticed, but also that it would maximize our chances for at least some of the group's escape if one of us should be discovered...a truly comforting thought.

Even though Luanna had claimed to have been watching for us at the Dispatcher's, it had been so long ago I fully expected her scent would have long since dissipated or at least been masked by the passage of numerous others. As such, I was moderately surprised when the werewolf signaled almost immediately that he had found the trail and headed off with a determined air. Either her scent was stronger than I had thought, or I had grossly underestimated Pepe's tracking ability.

The trail wound up and down the cobblestoned streets, and we followed as quickly as we could without abandoning our pretense of being casual strollers who did not know each other. For a while, our group made up the majority of the beings visible, causing me to doubt the effectiveness of our ruse, but soon the vampires began to emerge to indulge their taste for the nightlife and we became much less obvious.

I was paired up with Chumley, but the troll was strangely quiet as we made our way along. At first I thought he was simply concentrating on keeping the werewolf in sight, but as time wore on, I found the silence somehow unnerving. I had always respected Chumley as being one of the saner, leveler heads among our motley assemblage, and I was starting to have an uneasy impression that he was not wholeheartedly behind this venture.

"Is there something bothering you, Chumley?" I asked at last.

"Hmmm? Oh. Not really, Skeeve. I was just thinking."

"About what?"

The troll let out a small sigh.

"I was just contemplating our adversary, this Vic fellow. You know, from what's been said, he's quite resourceful in a devious sort of way."

That took me a little aback. So far I had considered our vampire foe to be everything from an annoyance to a nemesis. The idea of studying his methods had never entered my mind.

"What leads you to that conclusion?"

The troll pursed his lips as he organized his thoughts.

"Consider what he's accomplished so far. The entire time we've known of him, he's been on the run...first from the Deveels, and then from Aahz, who's no slouch at hunting people once he sets his mind to it. Now, assuming for the moment that Vic is actually the brains of the group, he was quick enough to take advantage of being left alone in your waiting room to escape out the back door. He couldn't have planned that in advance, even knowing about the door. He probably had some other plan in mind, and formulated this new course of action on the spot."

We paused for a moment to let a small group of vampires cross the intersection in front of us.

"Now, that would have sufficed for an escape in most instances, but they happened to pick an exit route that left you and Aahz responsible, which set your partner on their trail," Chumley continued. "With nothing to go on but your reputations, Vic not only correctly deduced that he would be followed, but he also managed to spot Aahz's weakness and exploit it to frame him and make it stick. . . again, not the easiest task, particularly realizing it involved convincing and coaching his two accomplices in their roles."

All of this was doing nothing for my peace of mind. I was having enough difficulty forcing myself to believe that we were really hunting a vampire, the sort of creature I normally avoid at all costs, without having to deal with the possibility that he was shrewd and re-sourceful as well. Still, I had learned that ignoring unpleasant elements of a caper was perhaps the worst way to prepare for them.

"Keep going," I urged.

"Well," the troll sighed, "when you stumbled on his hiding place at the Woof Writers, he didn't panic. He waited to hear as much of your plans as possible, all the while taking advantage of the opportunity to assess you first-hand, then timed his escape so as to catch you all flat-footed."

I digested this distasteful addition to the rapidly grow-ing data file. "Do you really think he was sizing me up?"

"There's no doubt in my mind. Not only was he

146

gauging your skills and determination, he was successful enough at second-guessing you, based on the results of his studies, to be waiting to sound the alarm when you busted Aahz out of jail....a particularly bold move when one realizes that he was running the risk of being recognized, which would have blown his frame-up of your partner."

"Bold or desperate," I said thoughtfully. "That's probably why he waited until we had actually sprung Aahz and were on the way down before he blew the whistle. If we had gotten away unscathed, then the frame would be useless, so at that point he really wasn't risking anything."

"Have it your way," the troll shrugged. "The final analysis remains that we have one tough nut to crack. One can only wonder what he will do when we catch up with him this time."

"If he's performing up to par, it could be rough on us."

Chumley shot me a sidelong glance.

"Actually, I was thinking it could be rough on your lady fair...if he has managed to observe the feelings you have for her."

I started to protest, then the impact of his theory hit me and my embarrassment gave way to concern.

"Is it really that apparent? Do you think he could spot it? If so, he might already have done something to Luanna for having contacted us."

"It stands out all over you to anyone who knows you," Chumley said, shaking his head. "As for someone watching you for the first time...I just don't know. He'd be more likely to deduce it from the information you had...such as his name. That kind of data had to come from somewhere, though there's an outside chance that with your current reputation he'll assume that you gleaned it by some magical source."

I barely heard him. My mind was focused on the possibility that Luanna might be hurt, and that I might indirectly have been the cause. A black well of guilt was rising up to swallow me, when I felt a hand on my shoulder.

"Don't tune out now, Skeeve," Chumley was saying, shaking me slightly. "First of all, we're going to need you shortly. Secondly, even if Vic's figured out that you're in love with her, I don't think he'll have hurt her. If anything, he'll save her for a trump card to use against us."

I drew a deep ragged breath.

". . .and he'll be just the bastard to do it, too," I said. "I don't know what I'll be able to do, for us or for her, but I'll be ready to try. Thanks, Chumley."

The troll was studying me closely.

"Actually, I wasn't thinking that he was such a blighter," he said. "More like a clever, resourceful person who's gotten in over his head and is trying his best to ad-lib his way out. Frankly, Skeeve old boy, in many ways he reminds me of you. You might think about that when attempting to appraise his likely courses of action and how to counter them."

I tried again to weigh what he was saying, but all I could think about was what the consequences of this hunt could mean to Luanna. It was difficult enough for me to accept that we would have to force Luanna and her cohorts to answer to the authorities for their indiscretions, but the thought of placing her in physical danger was unbearable.

I looked around for Aahz, fully intending to put an end to this hunt once and for all. To my surprise, the rest of the group was assembled on the corner ahead, and my partner was beckoning us to join them.

"What's going one?" I asked, almost to myself.

"Just off-hand," Chumley replied, "I'd say we've reached our destination."

A cold wave of fear washed over me, and I hurried to the rendezvous with Chumley close behind.

"We're in luck," Aahz announced as I arrived. "Guido here says he saw Vic entering the building just as we got here. It's my guess they're all inside right now."

"Aahz, I—I want us to quit right now," I blurted, painfully aware of how weak it sounded.

"Oh?" my partner said, cocking an eyebrow at me. "Any particular reason?"

I licked my lips, feeling the eyes of the whole group on me.

"Only one. I'm in love with one of the fugitives . . . the girl."

"Yeah. Now tell me something I didn't know," Aahz smirked, winking at me.

"You knew?"

"All of us knew. In fact, we were just discussing it. Remember, we all know you . . . and me probably best of all. It's already been pretty much decided to let your love-light go. Think of it as a present from us to you. The other two are ours."

Five minutes ago, that would have made me deliriously happy. Now, it only seemed to complicate things.

"But Chumley was just saying that there's a chance they might hurt her if they find out she helped us," I explained desperately. "Can't we just let them all go?"

"Not a chance, partner," Aahz said firmly. "In addition to our original reasons, you've just mentioned the new one. Your girlfriend could be in trouble, and the only way to be sure she's safe is to remove her partners . . . Fast."

"Believe him, Skeeve," Tananda urged. "It may not be nice, but it's the best way."

"Really, Boss," Guido said quietly. "Unless we finish this thing here and now, you're never goin' to know if she's safe, know what I mean?"

That almost made sense, but I was still worried. "I don't know, Aahz. . . ."

"Well I do," my partner snapped. "And the longer we stand down here, the more chance there is that they'll either get away or set up a trap. If you're uncertain, stay down here...in fact, that's not a bad idea. Massha, you stay down here with him in case they try to bolt out this way. While you're waiting, watch for the witnesses that Vilhelm's supposed to be sending along. Tananda, you and Chumley and Guido come along with me. This is a job for experienced hard-cases. Pepe, we appreciate your help, but this isn't really your fight."

"But of course." The werewolf grinned. "Besides, I am a lo-var, not a figh-tar. I will wait here to see the finale, eh?"

"But Aahz...."

"Really, partner, you'll be more help down here. This isn't your kind of fight, and we need someone to deal with the witnesses. You're good at that kind of thing."

"I was going to ask if you had given the signal to Vilhelm."

"Signal?" Aahz blinked. "How's this for a signal?!"

With that, he tore off his wig and threw it on the ground, followed closely by his dress.

"Think he'll get the message? Besides, no way am I going to try to fight in that get-up."

"Now you're talkin'!" Guido crowed.

In a flash he had discarded his cloak and was pulling on his now-familiar trench coat.

"Where did that come from?" I demanded.

"Had it with me all the time," the bodyguard said smugly. "It would have been like leaving an old friend behind."

"Well, if you and your old friend are ready," Tananda murmured, "we'd better get started."

"Itching for action?" Aahz grinned.

"No. More like eager to get off the street," she said. "Since you boys have shown your true colors, we're starting to draw a crowd."

Sure enough, the vampires on the street had ceased whatever they had been doing before and were gathering in knots, whispering together and pointing at our group.

"Umm...we'd better finish this fast," Aahz said, shooting a nervous glance around. "All right, gang. Let's go for the gusto!"

"Go for the what?" I asked, but they were already on their way into the building.

I noticed they were all moving faster than normal. I also noticed that Massha, Pepe, and I were the only ones left on the street...and now the crowd was pointing at us!

# Chapter XVIII

**"I didn't come all this way
to sit out the fight!"**

**R. Balboa**

WHAT'S going on?"

I looked around to find that one of the vampires had detached himself from his group of friends and was addressing me directly.

"Beats me," Massha interceded. "A bunch of off-worlder types just took off into that building with blood in their eyes. I'm waiting to see what happens next."

"Far out," the vampire breathed, peering toward the structure. "I haven't seen that many off-worlders in one place except in the flickers. Wasn't one of them that escaped murderer, Aahz?"

I really didn't want this character to join our little group. While our disguises seemed to be holding up under casual inspection, I was pretty sure that prolonged close scrutiny would reveal not only the non-local nature of Massha and myself, but also the fact that we were trying to hide it.

"You may be right," I said, playing a hunch. "If so, it's a good thing you happened along. We're going to need all the help we can get."

"Help? Help for what?"

"Why to catch the murderer, of course. We can't let him get away again. I figure it's our duty to stop him ourselves or at least slow him up until the authorities arrive."

"We? You mean the three of you? You're going to try to stop a murderer all by yourselves?"

"Four of us now that you're here."

The vampire started backing away.

"Ummm...actually I've got to get back to my friends. We're on our way to a party. Sorry I can't help, but I'll spread the word that you're looking for volunteers, okay?"

"Hey, thanks," I called as if I believed him. "We'll be right here."

By the time I had finished speaking, he had disappeared into the crowd. Mission accomplished.

"Nicely done, my friend," Pepe murmured. "He does not, how you say, want to get involved, no?"

"That's right," I said, my eyes on the building again. "And to tell you the truth, I'm not too wild about the idea either. What do you think, Massha? It's awfully quiet in there."

"I'll say," my apprentice agreed. "I'm just trying to figure out if that's a good or a bad sign. Another ten minutes and I'm heading in there to check it out myself."

I nodded my consent, even though I doubted she saw it. We both had our eyes glued to the building, memorizing its every detail.

It was a four-story structure...or it would be if it weren't for the curved peak that jutted out from the roof fully half-again as high as the main building. It looked as if the builder had suddenly added the adornment in a last-minute attempt to have his work stand as tall or taller than its neighbors. From the number of windows in the main structure, I guessed it was an apartment building or a hotel or something. In short, it looked like it had a lot of little rooms. I found myself wondering exactly how our

153

strike force was supposed to locate their target without kicking in every door in the place...a possibility I wouldn't put past Aahz.

I was about to express this fear to Massha when a loud crash sounded from within.

"What was that?" I demanded of no one in particular.

"Sounded like a loud crash," my apprentice supplied helpfully.

I forced myself to remember that no one out here knew any more about what was going on inside than I did.

After the crash, everything was quiet once more. I tried to tell myself that the noise might have nothing at all to do with the strike force, but I didn't believe it for a minute. The crowd was talking excitedly to each other and straining to see the various windows. They seemed quite confident that something else would happen soon, much more than I, but then again, maybe as city dwellers they were more accustomed to such vigils than I.

Suddenly, Tananda appeared in the doorway.

"Did they come out this way?" she called.

"No one's been in or out since you went in," I responded.

She swore and started to re-enter the building.

"What happened?" I shouted desperately.

"We nailed one of them, but Vic got away. He's loose in the building somewhere, and he's got the girl with him."

With that, she disappeared before I could make any further inquiries.

Terrific.

"Exciting, eh?" Pepe said. "I tell you, I could watch such a chase for hours."

"Well, I can't," I snapped. "I've had it with sitting on the sidelines. Massha? I'm going in there. Want to come?"

"I dunno, Hot Stuff. I'd like to, but somebody should be here to plug this escape route."

"Fine. You wait here, and I'll...."

I turned to enter the building and bumped headlong into Vilhelm.

"What are you doing here?" I demanded, not really caring.

The Dispatcher shook his head slightly to clear it. Being smaller, he had gotten the worse of our collision.

"I'm here with the witnesses, remember? I was supposed to bring them."

"You were supposed to *send* them. Oh well, where are they?"

"Right here," he said, gesturing to a sullen group of vampires standing behind him. "This is Kirby, and Paul, and Richard, and Adele, and Scott...some of the most respected citizens in town. Convince them and you're home free."

Looking at the group, I suddenly realized how Aahz had ended up on death row. If the jury had been anything like these specimens, they would have hung their own mothers for jaywalking. While I didn't relish the thought of trying to convince them of anything, I found myself being very glad I didn't have to deal with them on a regular basis.

"Okay. So we're here," the one identified as Kirby growled. "Just what is it we're supposed to be witnessing? If this is one of your cockamamie deals, Vilhelm...."

I interrupted simply by taking my sunglasses off and opening my eyes wide, displaying their whites. The bad reputation of humans in this dimension was sufficient to capture their undivided attention.

"Perhaps you recall a certain murder trial that took place not too long ago?" I said, trying to work the tooth-black off with my tongue. "Well, the convicted murderer who escaped is my partner, and right now he's inside that building. He and a few of our friends are about to show you one surprisingly lively corpse...specifically the fellow that my partner is supposed to have killed. I trust that will be sufficient to convince you of his innocence?"

While the vampires were taken aback by my presence in their midst, they recovered quickly. Like I said, they were real hard cases and didn't stay impressed very long.

"So how much time is this going to take?" Kirby said impatiently. "I'm giving up my sleep for this, and I don't get much of it."

That was a good question, so, not having an answer, I stalled.

"You sleep nights? I thought...."

"I'm a day owl," the vampire waved. "It's easier to get my work done when the phone isn't ringing every five minutes...which usually means waiting until everyone else is asleep. But we're getting off the subject. The bottom line is that my time is valuable, and the same holds true for my colleagues. If you think we're going to just stand around here until...."

There was a sudden outcry from the crowd, and we all looked to find them talking excitedly and pointing up at the roof.

A figure had emerged, fighting to pick his way across the steeply sloped surface while dragging a struggling girl by one arm.

Vic!

This was the first time I had gotten a clear look at my foe, and I was moderately surprised. He was younger than I had expected, barely older than myself, and instead of a menacing cloak, he was sporting a white turtleneck and sunglasses. It suddenly occurred to me that if sunglasses enabled me to pass for a vampire, that they would also let a vampire pass undetected among humans.

The vampire suddenly stopped as his path was barred by Tananda, who appeared as if by magic over the edge of the roof. He turned to retrace his steps, only to find that the trio of Aahz, Guido, and Chumley had emerged behind him, cutting off his retreat.

"I believe, gentlemen and lady, that up there is the elusive body that started this whole thing," I heard myself saying. "If you can spare a few more moments, I think *my* colleagues will have him in custody so that you might interrogate him at your leisure."

"Don't be too sure of that, High Roller," Massha cautioned. "Look!"

His chosen routes of escape cut off, Vic was now scrabbling up the roof peak itself, Luanna hanging in his grip. While I had to admire his strength, I was at a loss to understand what he was trying to accomplish with the manuever. It was obvious that he had been exposed, so why didn't he just give it up?

The answer became apparent in the next few moments. Reaching the apex of the roof, the vampire underwent a chilling metamorphosis. Before the strike force could reach him, he hunched forward and huge batwings began to grow and spread from his back. His plans gone awry, he was getting ready to escape.

In immediate response to his efforts, Tananda and Guido both produced projectile weapons and shouted something to him. Though the distance was too great to make out the words clearly, it was obvious to me that they were threatening to shoot him down if he tried to take to the air.

"We may have a murder case yet," Kirby murmured, squinting to watch the rooftop drama unfold.

"Murder?" I exclaimed, turning on him. "How can you call it murder if they're only trying to keep from escaping *your* justice?"

"That wasn't what I meant," the vampire said, never taking his eyes from the action. "Check it out."

I looked...and my heart stood still.

Aahz had been trying to ease up the roof peak closer to Vic and his hostage. Vic must have seen him, because he was now holding Luanna out over the drop as he pointed an angry finger at my partner. The threat was unmistakable.

"You know, eet is people like zat who give ze vampires

157

a bad name, eh?" Pepe said, nudging me.

I ignored him, lost in my own anxiety and frustration at the stalemated situation. A noticeably harder jab from Massha broke my reverie, however.

"Hey, Hot Stuff. Do you see what I see?"

I tore my gaze away from the confrontation and shot a glance her way. She was standing motionless, her brow furrowed with concentration and her eyes closed.

It took me a few moments to realize what she was doing, then I followed suit, scarcely daring to hope.

There it was! A force line! A big, strong, beautiful, glorious force line.

I had gotten so used to not having any magical energy at my disposal in this dimension that I hadn't even bothered to check!

I opened myself to the energy, relished it for a fleet moment, then rechanneled it.

"Excuse me," I said with a smile, handing my sunglasses to Kirby. "It's about time I took a hand in this directly."

With that, I reached out with my mind, pushed off against the ground, and soared upward, setting a course for the cornered vampire on the roof.

©PFoglio '84

# Chapter XIX

*"All right, pilgrim.*
*This is between you and me!"*
**A. Hamilton**

I had hoped to make my approach unobserved, but as I flew upward, the crowd below let out a roar that drew the attention of the combatants on the roof. Terrific! When I wanted unobtrusive, I got notoriety.

Reaching a height level with that of the vampire, I hovered at a discreet distance.

"Put away the nasties," I called to Tananda and Guido. "He's not getting away by air."

They looked a bit rebellious, but followed the order.

"What's with the Peter Pan bit, partner?" Aahz shouted. "Are you feeling your Cheerioats, or did you finally find a force line?"

"Both." I waved back, then turned my attention to Vic.

Though his eyes were obscured by his sunglasses, I could feel his hateful glare burning into me to the bone.

"Why don't you just call it quits?" I said in what I hoped was a calm, soothing tone. "It's over. We've got you outflanked."

For a moment he seemed to waiver with indecision.

Then, without warning, he threw Luanna at Aahz.

"Why can't you all just leave me alone!" he screamed, and dove off the roof.

Aahz somehow managed to snag the girl's hurtling form, though in the process he lost his balance and tumbled backward down the roof peak, cushioning the impact with his own body.

I hesitated, torn between the impulse to check on Luanna's welfare and the desire to pursue Vic.

"Go get him!" my partner called. "We're fine!"

That was all the encouragement I needed. Wheeling to my right, I plunged after the fleeing vampire.

What followed was one of the more interesting experiences of my limited magical career. As I mentioned before, my form of flying magically isn't really flying. . .it's controlled levitation of oneself. This made enthusiastic pursuit a real challenge to my abilities. To counterbalance the problem, however, Vic couldn't really fly either. . .at least he never seemed to flap his wings. Instead, he appeared content to soar and bank and catch an occasional updraft. This forced him to continually circle and double back through roughly the same area time and time again. This suited me fine, as I didn't want to wander too far away from my energizing force line now that I had found it. The idea of running out of power while suspended fifty feet in the air did not appeal to me at all.

Anyway, our aerial duel rapidly became a curious matching of styles with Vic's swooping and circling in his efforts to escape and my vertical and horizontal maneuverings to try to intercept him. Needless to say, the conflict was not resolved quickly. As soon as I would time a move that came close enough to an interception to justify attempting it again, Vic would realize his danger and alter his pattern, leaving me to try to puzzle out his new course.

The crowd loved it.

They whooped and hollered, their words of encouragement alternately loud and faint as we changed altitude.

161

It was impossible to tell which of us they were cheering for, though for a while I thought it was me, considering the approval they had expressed when I first took off to join the battle. Then I noticed that the crowd was considerably larger than it had been when I entered the fray, and I realized that many of them had not been around to witness the beginning of the conflict. To them, it probably appeared that a monster from another dimension was chasing one of their fellow beings through the sky.

That thought was disquieting enough that I spared some of my attention to scan the surrounding rooftops on the off-chance that a local sniper might be preparing to help his fellow countryman. It turned out to be the wisest decision I had made.

As I was looking over my shoulder, I plowed full force into Vic, who had doubled back on his own path. The feint would have probably worked if I had seen it, but as it was we collided at maximum speed, the impact momentarily stunning us both. I managed to grab a double handful of the vampire's turtleneck as we fell about ten feet before I adjusted my levitation strength to support us both.

"What's the matter with you!" I demanded, trying to shake him, which succeeded only in moving us both back and forth in the air. "Running away won't help."

Then I realized he was crying.

Somehow, this struck me as immensely unfair. I mean, how are you supposed to stay mad at a villain that cries? Okay. So I'm a soft tough. But the crying really did make a difference.

"I can't fight you all!" he sobbed, tears streaming down his cheeks. "Maybe if I knew some magic I could take one of you with me...but at least you're going to have to work for your kill!"

With that he tore loose from my grasp and swooped away.

His words stunned me so much I almost let him escape. Fortunately, I had the presence of mind to call out to him.

"Hey, dummy! Nobody's trying to kill you!"

"Yeah, sure," he shouted back. "You're up here just for the fun of it."

He was starting to bank toward the street, and I knew I'd only have time for one more try.

"Look! Will you stop running if I quit chasing you? I think there's a major misunderstanding here."

He glanced back over his shoulder and saw that I was still where I was when we collided. Altering his course slightly, he flared his wings and landed on a carved gargoyle ornament jutting out from the side of the building.

"Why should you want to talk?" he called, wiping his face with one hand. "I thought nothing I could say would change your mind."

"You'd be surprised," I shouted back. "Say, do you mind if I land on that ledge near you? I feel pretty silly just hanging here."

He glanced at the indicated ledge, and I could see his wings flex nervously.

"C'mon," I urged. "I'll be further away from you there than I was when we started this chase back on the roof. You'll still have a clean shot at getting away if I try anything."

He hesitated, then nodded his consent.

Moving slowly so as not to alarm him, I maneuvered my way to my new perch. Truth to tell, I was glad to get something solid under my feet again. Even using magic, flying can take a lot out of you, and I was relieved to get a chance to rest. Now that I was closer, I could see that Vic was breathing heavily himself. Apparently his form of flying was no picnic either.

"All right," I said in a much more conversational tone. "Let's take this thing from the top. Who says we're trying to kill you?"

"Matt does," the vampire responded. "He's the one who filled me in on you and your pet demon. To be honest with you, I had never even heard of you until Matt explained whose home we had stumbled into."

"Matt?" I frowned.

Then I remembered. Of course. The third member of the fugitive party. Luanna's old con artist partner who nobody had been paying attention to at all. A germ of an idea began to form in my head.

"And he says we're out to kill you?"

"That's right. According to him nobody crosses the Great Skeeve or makes a fool of him and lives . . . and using your house as an escape route definitely qualifies.

The reputation thing again. I was beginning to realize why so many magicians preferred to lead the lives of recluses.

"That's crazy, Vic." I said. "If I tried to kill everybody who's made a fool of me, I'd be armpit-deep in corpses."

"Oh yeah?" he shot back. "Well, if you aren't out to kill me, why did you send your pet demon after us?"

Despite my resolve to settle this thing amicably, I was starting to get annoyed.

"First of all, he's not my pet demon. He's my partner and his name is Aahz. Secondly, I didn't send him. He knocked me out cold and came himself. Third and final, he was never out to kill you. He was trying to bring you and your cohorts back to Deva so we wouldn't get stuck paying off the people you swindled plus a hefty fine. Are you getting all this, or am I going too fast for you?"

"But I didn't swindle anybody," the vampire protested. "Those two offered me a job helping them sell magic charms. I didn't know they weren't genuine until Matt said the customers were mad and we had to run. I suggested we hide out here because it's the only place I know besides the Bazaar."

"Uh-huh," I said, studying the sky. "Next you'll be saying you didn't frame my partner *or* sound the alarm on us when we tried to spring him."

Vic's wings dropped as he hung his head.

"That much I can't deny . . . but I was scared! I

framed the demon because it was the only way I could think of to get him off our trail for a while. I really thought he could get loose on his own, and when I saw you at the Woof Writers', I knew he was going to get away. I sounded the alarm hoping you would all get caught and be detained long enough to give us a head start. Looking back on it, they were pretty ratty things to do, but what would *you* do if you had a pack of killer demons on your trail?"

Now *that* I could identify with. Chumley's words about Vic and I being alike echoed in my ears. I had had to improvise in some pretty hairy situations myself.

"Wait a minute!" I growled. "Speaking of killer demons, what was that bit with you dangling Luanna over the edge of the building back there?"

"I was bluffing," the vampire shrugged. "Your friends were threatening to shoot me if I tried to fly away, and it was the only thing I could think of to try to get them to back off. I wouldn't deliberately hurt anyone...especially Luanna. She's sweet. That's why I was trying to help her escape with me after they caught Matt."

That brought me to the question that had been nagging at my mind since I started this wild chase.

"If you don't mind me asking, why didn't you just change into mist and drift away? We could never have caught you then."

Vic gave a short, bitter laugh.

"Do you know how rough it is to turn into mist? Well, you're a magician. Maybe you do know. Anyway, you might as well know the truth. I'm not much in the magic department...in fact, I'm pretty much a bust as a vampire. I can't even change all the way into a bat! These wings are the best I've been able to do. That's why I was looking for a new life in the Bazaar. I'd rather be a first-class anything than a third-rate vampire. I mean, I don't even like blood!"

"You should meet my bodyguard." I grinned despite myself. "He's a gangster who's allergic to garlic."

"Garlic? I love garlic."

I opened my mouth to offer him Guido's job, then shut it rapidly. If this character was half as desperate as he sounded, he'd probably take the offer seriously and accept, and then where would I be? All we needed to complete our menagerie was a magic-poor vampire.

"Well," I said instead, "I guess that answers all my questions except one. Now that you know we aren't trying to kill you, are you ready to quit running and face the music?"

The vampire gnawed his lower lip as he thought.

"You're sure it will be all right?"

"I can't say for sure until I talk to my partner," I admitted, "but I'm pretty sure things will be amenable. The main problem is to get the murder charges against him dropped . . . which I think we've already accomplished. As for you, I think the only thing they could have against you is false arrest, and there's no way Aahz will press charges on that one."

"Why not?"

I gave him my best grin.

"Because if he did, we couldn't take you back to Deva to deal with the swindling charge. Believe me, if given a chance between revenge and saving money, you can trust Aahz to be forgiving every time."

Vic thought about it for a few more moments, then shrugged.

"Embarrassment I'm used to dealing with, and I think I can beat the swindling rap. C'mon, Skeeve. Let's get this thing over with."

Having finally reached a truce, however temporary, we descended together to face the waiting crowd.

# Chapter XX

*"There's no accounting for taste!"*
**Colonel Sanders**

BUT Skeeve...."

BANG!

"...I told you before...."

BANG! BANG!

"...I could never abandon Matt...."

BANG!

"...he's my partner!"

BANG! BANG!

"But Lu...."

BANG!

"...excuse me. HEY, PARTNER! COULD YOU KNOCK OFF THE HAMMERING FOR A MINUTE? I'M TRYING TO HAVE A CONVERSATION HERE!"

"Not a chance," Aahz growled around his mouthful of nails. "I'm shutting this door permanently before anything else happens. But tell you what, I'll try to hammer quietly."

If you deduce from all this that we were back at our place on Deva, you're right. After some long, terse conversations with the citizens of Blut and fond farewells to Vilhelm and Pepe, our whole crew, including our three captives, had trooped back to the castle and through the door without incident.

I had hoped to have a few moments alone with Luanna, but, after several attempts, the best I had been able to manage was this conversation in the reception room under the watchful eyes of Aahz and Matt.

Matt, incidentally, turned out to be a thoroughly unpleasant individual with a twisted needle-nose, acne, a receding hairline, and the beginnings of a beer-belly. For the life of me, I couldn't figure out what Luanna saw in him.

"But that was when you thought he was in a jam," I said, resuming the argument. "Aahz and I have already promised to help defend him *and* Vic when they go before the Merchants Association. There's no need to stand by him yourself."

"I don't understand you, Skeeve," Luanna declared, shaking her head. "If I wouldn't leave Matt when he was in trouble, why should I leave him when things look like they're going to turn out okay? I know you don't like him, but he's done all right by me so far...and I still owe him for getting me away from the farm."

"But we're making you a good offer," I tried again desperately. "You can stay here and work for Aahz and I, and if you're interested we could even teach you some real magic so you don't have to...."

She stopped me by simply laying a hand on my arm.

"I know it's a good offer, Skeeve, and it's nice of you to make it. But for the time being I'm content to stay with Matt. Maybe sometime in the future, when I have a little more to offer you in return, I'll take you up on it...if the deal's still open."

"Well," I sighed, "if that's really what you want...."

"Hey! Don't take it so hard, buddy," Matt laughed, clapping his hand on my shoulder. "You win some, you lose some. This time you lost. No hard feelings. Maybe you'll have better luck with the next one. We're both men of the world, and we know one broad's just like any other."

"Matt, *buddy*," I said through clenched teeth, "get that hand off my shoulder before it loses a body."

As I said, even on our short trip back from Limbo I had been so underwhelmed by Matt that I no longer even bothered trying to be polite or mask my dislike for him. He could grate on my nerves faster than anyone I had ever met. If he was a successful con artist, able to inspire trust from total strangers, then I was the Queen of May.

"Matt's just kidding," Luanna soothed, stepping between us.

"Well I'm not," I snarled. "Just remember you're welcome here any time you get fed up with this slug."

"Oh, I imagine we'll be together for quite some time," Matt leered, patting Luanna lightly on her rump. "With you big shots vouching for us we should be able to beat this swindling rap. . .and even if we lose, so what? All it means is I'll have to give them back their crummy twenty gold pieces."

Aahz's hammering stopped abruptly. . .or maybe it was my heart.

I tried vainly to convince myself that I hadn't heard him right.

"Twenty gold pieces?" I said slowly.

"Yeah. They caught on to us a lot quicker here at the Bazaar than I thought they would. It wasn't much of a haul even by my standards. I can't get over the fact that you big shots went through so much trouble to drag us back here over a measly twenty gold pieces. There must be more to this principle thing than I realized."

"Ummm. . .could I have a word with you, partner?" Aahz said, putting down his hammer.

"I was about to ask the same thing," I admitted, stepping to the far side of the room.

Once we were alone, we stared at each other, neither wanting to be the first to speak.

"You never did get around to asking Hay-ner how much was at stake, did you?" Aahz sighed absently.

"That's the money side of negotiations and I thought you covered it," I murmured. "Funny, we both stood right there the whole time and heard every word that was said, and neither of us caught that omission."

"Funny. Right. I'm dying." My partner grimaced.

"Not as much as you will if word of this gets out," I warned. "I vote that we give them the money to pay it off. I don't want to , but it's the only way I can think of to keep this thing from becoming public knowledge."

"Done." Aahz nodded. "But let me handle it. If Matt the Rat there gets wind of the fact that the whole thing was a mistake on our part, he'd probably blackmail us for our eyeteeth."

"Right," I agreed.

With that, we, the two most sought-after, most highly-paid magicians at the Bazaar, turned to deal with our charges, reminded once more why humility lies at the core of greatness.